## "My boots!"

Jaycie burst through the doorway, thundering to the rescue of her prized cowboy boots.

Cub gaped at the small girl. He looked as stunned as if he'd been kicked in the head by a bull.

Alyssa met his gaze. "Congratulations, Cub Goodacre, you're a father."

All but one corner of his mind went numb. He didn't know the first thing about children. He was a cowboy, damn it. No way could he be a—
"A what?"

"A father," she repeated.

"My boots!" The toddler strained pudgy fingers toward the boots in his white-knuckled grasp.

"You mean this is—"

"Mine!" the child demanded.

"Yours," Alyssa declared.

Joy rose to mingle with a pain so fierce it registered as heat in Cub's chest. Despite the sudden stirrings of parental emotion, something in him shuddered.

A life-scarred loner like him had no business being a father....

Dear Reader,

This month, Romance is chock-full of excitement. First, VIRGIN BRIDES continues with *The Bride's Second Thought*, an emotionally compelling story by bestselling author Elizabeth August. When a virginal bride-to-be finds her fiancé with another woman, she flees to the mountains for refuge...only to be stranded with a gorgeous stranger who gives her second thoughts about a lot of things....

Next, Natalie Patrick offers up a delightful BUNDLES OF JOY with *Boot Scootin' Secret Baby*. Bull rider Jacob "Cub" Goodacre returns to South Dakota for his rodeo hurrah, only to learn he's still a married man...and father to a two-year-old heart tugger. BACHELOR GULCH, Sandra Steffen's wonderful Western series, resumes with the story of an estranged couple who had wed for the sake of their child...but wonder if they can rekindle their love in *Nick's Long-Awaited Honeymoon*.

Rising star Kristin Morgan delivers a tender, sexy tale about a woman whose biological clock is booming and the best friend who consents to being her *Shotgun Groom*. If you want a humorous—red-hot!—read, try Vivian Leiber's *The 6'2", 200 lb. Challenge*. The battle of the sexes doesn't get any better! Finally, Lisa Kaye Laurel's fairy-tale series, ROYAL WEDDINGS, draws to a close with *The Irresistible Prince*, where the woman hired to find the royal a wife realizes *she* is the perfect candidate!

In May, VIRGIN BRIDES resumes with Annette Broadrick, and future months feature titles by Suzanne Carey and Judy Christenberry, among others. So keep coming back to Romance, where you're sure to find the classic tales you love, told in fresh, exciting ways.

Enjoy!

*Joan Marlow Golan*

Joan Marlow Golan
Senior Editor, Silhouette Romance

---

Please address questions and book requests to:
Silhouette Reader Service
U.S.: 3010 Walden Ave., P.O. Box 1325, Buffalo, NY 14269
Canadian: P.O. Box 609, Fort Erie, Ont. L2A 5X3

# BOOT SCOOTIN'
# SECRET BABY

## Natalie Patrick

*Silhouette*
R O M A N C E™
Published by Silhouette Books
**America's Publisher of Contemporary Romance**

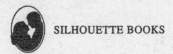 SILHOUETTE BOOKS

ISBN 0-373-19289-4

BOOT SCOOTIN' SECRET BABY

Copyright © 1998 by Luanne Jones

This edition published by arrangement with Harlequin Books S.A.

® and TM are trademarks of Harlequin Books S.A., used under license. Trademarks indicated with ® are registered in the United States Patent and Trademark Office, the Canadian Trade Marks Office and in other countries.

Printed in U.S.A.

**Books by Natalie Patrick**

Silhouette Romance

*Wedding Bells and Diaper Pins* #1095
*The Marriage Chase* #1130
*Three Kids and a Cowboy* #1235
*Boot Scootin' Secret Baby* #1289

## NATALIE PATRICK

believes in romance and has firsthand experience to back up that belief. She met her husband in January and married him in April of that same year—they would have eloped sooner, but friends persuaded them to have a real wedding. Ten years and two children later, she knows she's found her real romantic hero.

Amid the clutter in her work space, she swears that her headstone will probably read: "She left this world a brighter place but not necessarily a cleaner one." She certainly hopes her books brighten her readers' days.

Bundles
of Joy

Dear Reader,

Ah, the terrible twos. I remember them well—from my children's toddlerhood, not my own. Me? I'm sure I was every inch an angel, unlike little boot scootin' Jaycie Goodacre. Cub and Alyssa really have their hands full with that one, and I wish, as an experienced mom, I could give them some sage advice.

But honestly, I don't recall either of my children being any more "terrible" at two than at one or at three or what have you. Maybe I'm seeing things through a sentimental haze—or maybe by comparison to their current preteen years, I have come to appreciate the open curiosity, the unbridled enthusiasm, the strident quest for self-determination…and the long afternoon naps of my children's toddler days.

So, I think in the end the only advice I would give Alyssa and Cub is to love their child and each other and to savor these times—because before they know it, Jaycie will be asking for the keys to Daddy's brand-new pickup truck!

*Natalie Patrick*

# *Prologue*

Dear Cub,

Come home.

Didn't you swear to me that when you'd won enough money bull riding to buy a ranch and settle down, you'd be back? Almost three years have passed since then, Cub. Your riding has made you darned near a legend. So, when will you come home?

I need to see you again. I need to look you in the eye and say the thousand and one things that I've stored in my heart since that horrible argument. A thousand things that can be distilled to only two—I love you, Cub Goodacre, and goodbye.

For so long I wanted you to come back so we

could try to work things out. I can no longer hope for that. I've moved on with my life.

Though I realize I will always love you in that wild, intense way that so suits a reckless cowboy like you, I have to let go of the dream that we could ever become equal partners in a relationship. I want nothing less than that and you want—well, you want what *you* want.

You wanted someone to shelter and protect, someone to take care of. I wanted the chance to become my own person, a person respected for her hard work, intelligence and generous heart.

I am that person today. I'm a new woman about to begin a whole new life, to take another chance at making it on my own. And in a funny way— funny in that way that could almost break your heart—you, Cub, *did* help me to become this confident woman, ready to take on the world.

My one regret is that you don't even know about the source of my inspiration, our two-year-old daughter, Jayne Cartwright Goodacre, or Jaycie as we all call her.

No. I take that back. I refuse to go into this new and exciting phase of my life with any regrets holding me back, tying me to you. That's why I wish you would come back, for closure and so I can let you know about the precious life our brief love created.

Yes, I tried at first to contact you, to let you know about your child. I tried desperately. But you had taken to the rodeo circuit like fire through a dry patch. I had always just missed you and you just kept moving on. I knew when I did finally manage to get through to you and you returned my letters unopened that you were trying to pay me back. If you had just opened one of those letters you might have forgiven me and we might...

But that time has passed. I don't want your forgiveness anymore. I don't need it.

On the day of Jaycie's birth, I only had to look in her eyes to know it was time to stop living for a man who simply wasn't there for us and start living for myself, my daughter and our future.

What will I tell our daughter when she is old enough to ask about her father? I think this, Cub—that her father was a good man with a great capacity to love but a very narrow definition of what that meant. A man who did not understand that one partner could not grow tall and strong if always in the protective shade of the other partner. He thought he could save me from my own mistakes—and that was the biggest mistake of all.

What will I tell myself each evening when I kiss our baby good-night and climb in bed alone? That I am strong and smart and do not need you or anyone to smooth my path for me. I can make my own way and be a proud example for our child.

Alyssa Cartwright scrawled her name across the bottom of the page, then laid her pen aside and slumped back in her chair.

She blinked to clear the dampness from her eyes. She would not cry. This was a time for celebration, not tears. Tomorrow marked her very own independence day.

Slowly, she turned the pale yellow paper over to admire the other side, her first PR job for her new partnership with Crowder and Cartwright, Western Management Company. Yes, it *had* been a publicity flyer for her parents' famous kick-off party for the Summit City Rodeo Days. But then, how better to prove her skill than by satisfying the people who doubted her capabilities most?

Both Yip and Dolly Cartwright had agreed that this was the very best flyer, bar none, ever done to announce their enormous barbecue. Of course they felt that way; not because their daughter had done the work, but because she had used their granddaughter, their pride and joy, as the model.

Alyssa swept one fingertip over the adorable picture of her baby, stroking the big black hat on Jaycie's head. Her finger skimmed over the bandanna that fell over the baby's bare chest and round belly, then brushed over the white diaper with cowboy-gun pins holding it up. Then she reached the boots. Cub's boots.

He'd left those boots behind the day he, for all intents and purposes, walked out of their marriage. Alyssa traced the outline of the boots right down to the nick in the heel, the nick he'd asked her to have repaired. Asked? Make that told—just like he told her everything.

"I went in with Price Wellman and bought us a ranch," he told her the day they'd arrived back from their short honeymoon. Then he'd said, "I've rented us a house to stay in until the deal goes through and we can build our own ranch house."

Two months later, he told her, "Price got busted up bad in a bull-riding wreck. He can't throw in with us on the ranch."

What Alyssa had seen as an opportunity for her to contribute to the marriage and to Cub's dream he had seen as another time to tell her how he saw things. "No wife of mine will have a job in town, especially not waitressing for love-starved cowboys. A good bull rider makes good money, darlin'. I know I promised I'd quit if you'd marry me, but looks like I got to take on one more season, maybe two. Then we can buy us a ranch outright and be set.''

She'd tried to tell him a thing or two, like the fact that she suspected she might be pregnant, but he didn't give her that chance. She'd never stood a chance, for that matter, when Cub took her in his arms. They'd made wild passionate love that night and in the morning, he'd left a note telling her to get the boots repaired and saying he'd call later.

She wasn't there to take his call, or any of his calls until he tracked her down at her parents' home.

Alyssa shut her eyes to blot out the memory of the horrible argument they'd had then, of the terrible threat she'd made to nullify their marriage, the threat that led Cub to tell her one last thing.

"Everything I've done, I've done for you and the good of our future. If you can't see that, then I guess I've let you down. I guess you have a right to want to be rid of me. You do what you have to do. You get your rich, famous daddy to pull strings and get a paper that says our marriage isn't real. I'll abide by the law of it, even if I never accept it in my heart. And I will promise you this—I'm coming home to you, Alyssa Goodacre, coming home a success, worthy of a woman like you, or I ain't comin' home at all.''

The words rang just as clear in her mind as they had when he first spoke them, and cut just as deep. Alyssa swallowed hard and turned her attention to the picture again. Cub hadn't come home and though she doubted he would ever show his face in Summit City again, some part of her hoped—

Well, why else would she use *his* boots on *his* daughter in an advertisement every rodeo rider haunting this part of the circuit would see? Why else would she pen her farewell to him on the back of one of those flyers?

She plucked the paper up from the writing desk and went out onto the balcony just off her bedroom.

The stars twinkled above in the black velvet of the South Dakota sky. The brisk wind thrashed at her hair. She drew in the crisp scent of late summer and gazed out at the bustling preparations still in full swing for her parents' barbecue tomorrow evening.

Tonight, she thought, she still lived at home, still felt like the gangly child who could never learn the riding and roping tricks that were her parents' stock-in-trade. Tonight she was still the girl who had one time disobeyed her father's edict "Love any boy but a cowboy, marry any man but a rodeo man," and had paid the price with her heart, her future and her self-esteem.

But come tomorrow that would all be behind her. Tomorrow, she would set herself on the path that would lead to success and financial independence. In a few months she'd have the money to move with her child into their own home. Nothing was going to stop her from building a terrific future. Especially not the past.

She lifted the paper; it cracked in the wind once, tore away from her fingers and went sailing into the night. She watched it somersault away, then whispered one last time the words she hoped her husband would someday hear, so she could finally close this chapter in her life. "Come home."

# Chapter One

Y'all Come!
Summit County Rodeo Days Kickoff Celebration
Bar-B-Que
Yahoo Buckaroo Western Ranch and Rodeo
Museum
Home of legendary rodeo show people, Yip and
Dolly Cartwright

Cub Goodacre narrowed his eyes at the flyer taped in the grimy front window of the Summit City Feed and Grain. His gaze skimmed past the particulars of the event—he knew how to get to the ranch, knew the glorified "goat roast" raged from early afternoon until the big fireworks shebang just after dark. He also knew that the invitation, extended to any and all with a love of the rodeo and ten dollars to spare for a ticket, did not include him.

A fist seemed to grip at his heart and slowly it began

to twist, tightening its searing hold with every beat. For almost three years, he'd stayed clear of the Summit City Rodeo Days and the painful memories it evoked. Now fate and his long-left-empty dreams had dragged him right back here to the scene of his proudest triumph and greatest devastation.

He blew out a long puff of warm air through his nostrils. His gaze dropped to the caption below the photo in the center of the yellow paper.

"You bet your boots, I'll be there, pardner!"

"Not me, kid," he muttered to the pint-size cowboy wanna-be peeking from under a black hat. "So just keep your boo—"

He froze smack-dab in the middle of turning his back on his past and the invitation to ride hell-for-leather back into it.

*My boots.* His lips moved but no sound came. He leaned down to get a better look at the black leather and snakeskin boots they'd let some diaper desperado use as a plaything.

His boots. No doubt about it. He could tell they were his by the jagged notch in the right heel. He'd left those damaged boots behind the last time he'd left Summit City.

He set his jaw and clamped his hands on his hips. The cool fabric of his faded jeans chafed his legs as his senses pricked up. He inhaled the crisp fall air and glared at the boots until he almost expected to burn a hole in the paper.

This picture could be the work of only one person— the only person he'd trusted with his favorite boots, the same person he'd trusted with his heart. She'd kept both of them.

Her image flashed like heat lightning scoring through his thoughts. Despite the years and the world of hurt between them, he still pictured her as she looked on their first date. Her strawberry-blond hair, pulled back in a single thick braid, fell from the crown of her head to square between her shoulder blades. He could even see the faint freckles sprinkled over her blushing cheeks and the sincerity and adoration shining in her hazel eyes.

How quickly that adoration had hardened to accusation, he realized in one flickering moment. He hadn't seen her face during their last, hateful argument, but he didn't have to. He'd heard the depth of her disappointment with him, the anger he'd hoped to avoid by leaving as he did, coming full force through the telephone lines.

His blood pounded in his veins like the thundering hooves of a bull gone loco. Cub forced his gaze back to the taunting advertisement. His cheek ticked as he struggled to control any outward show of the wild rush of emotions spinning in his chest, fighting to kick free.

This poster, this picture, this personal hell of his were all the work of one woman—Alyssa Cartwright.

The fancy logo at the center bottom of the paper confirmed it. Crowder and Cartwright Western Management Company, with a local address.

This had to mean she still lived in Summit City— probably still lived under her parents' roof, and under their thumb. And that meant she would probably show up at the rodeo.

*I promise you this—I'm coming home to you, Alyssa Goodacre, coming home a success, worthy of a woman like you, or I ain't comin' home at all.* His own words jeered him from his callow past. He'd become a success by most men's measure of the term, and now he'd finally come back to Alyssa's home, but there was one thing he couldn't claim. His time alone and a cruel trick of fate had taught him this: he was not now, nor could he likely ever be, worthy of the only woman he would ever ask to share his name. A man like him could only let her down and hurt her.

He hadn't come back to Summit City to prove something to Alyssa, though that dream had died hard. He'd come here now to prove something to himself.

Cub thought of the two rides he had remaining before he walked away from the rodeo forever—provided he could still walk by then. He shifted his weight to his right hip, then winced at the lingering pain from his last punishing ride. Two rides, win or lose, stood between him and walking away from bull riding like a man. If he didn't make those rides, he'd feel like a total failure. He'd failed as a son, as a protector, a champion, and a husband; he would not fail at the one thing he did right and that meant making those two rides.

Two rides. And Alyssa was going to be in the stands watching his next one.

How the hell was he supposed to concentrate with that on his mind and all these feelings he'd thought he'd buried churning up in his gut?

He couldn't.

So, he had just ten days to either get that gal out of his system or buffalo her into avoiding the rodeo on the night he rode. That meant that one way or another he had to see his ex-wife—and he'd prefer to do it on his own terms. But how?

"Cub?"

The sound of his name shot through his cluttered thoughts, making him flinch. Jerking his head around, he found a young girl standing beside him on the sidewalk.

She smiled, cocking her head so that her stark yellow hair swung down to brush over her equally artificial-looking cleavage.

He racked his brain to think how he could know this pretty young thing. He'd had his wild days, for sure. His "every good ride deserves another" philosophy defined many a post-rodeo celebration. However, from the moment he'd laid eyes on Alyssa to this day he'd never done more than collect his winnings and drive on to the next rodeo—or back to see her, when they'd dated.

The brilliant sun warmed the broad back of his dark shirt. He searched his memory for any trace of this girl's face but only one woman's face had ever been etched in his being. Carved with a knife that cut so deep the scars would never heal, he thought, fighting down his gut response.

He forced his attention back to the breathless blonde. From the looks of her now, this girl couldn't have been more than a teen in his own carousing days. And that was one line Cub didn't cross.

On his own since he was sixteen, he knew how easily a young person, hungry for love and acceptance, might latch onto someone older, longing to connect for a week, a day, even an hour, just to pretend he belonged, that someone gave a damn about him. But the people hanging on the fringe of the rodeo cared only for themselves and the next good time; he had learned that the hard way himself with an older version of this gal.

He half winced at the anxious girl waiting so close that he could hear the rasp of her shirt against his sleeve with every heave of her breasts. "I'm sorry, I don't recall meeting—"

"Oh, you don't know me." Her words rushed out like a brook undammed. "I'm a real big fan of yours. I recognized you by your hat."

He touched his thumb and forefinger to the brim of his trademark hat. He'd spent his first prize money to have one like it custom-made in Austin, Texas—cattleman's crown, Aussie brim—the kind that dipped down in front to always shade his eyes. He still had them made there, always in a deep smoked brown with a thin braided leather band, its ends hanging off the back just enough to whip in the air when he rode a killer bull.

"I was so excited when I heard you'd be riding here, especially since you haven't ridden here in a while," the girl gushed on. "But I knew you'd show up here to ride Diablo's Heartbreak."

At the mention of the bull he'd been dueling all season, Cub's lips twitched into what passed for him as a smile. "Sounds like you *are* a fan."

"How could I not be? I mean it's so exciting how you and Diablo's Heartbreak have been battling it out. One ride you show him who's boss and the next he tosses you right on—"

"My assessment differs somewhat, ma'am. But I get your point." He nodded his head, his jaw tight at the reminder that he had yet to really best the beast. "Now if you don't mind, I've got unfinished business to attend to."

"Oh." She blinked as though she'd expected more. "Um, well, um, could you…could you sign this?"

He half expected her to offer her breast for his signature but when he glanced down he saw a flyer, just like the one in the window, and a pen thrust out toward him. He took the page and carefully lettered his name in his blocky penmanship that some cowboy once said looked like it had been spelled out with western cattle brands instead of written by a man.

"There." He handed the flyer back to the woman, who clearly was not pleased.

Well, that was his lot in life—letting women down. He hadn't been able to save his own mother from a life with an abusive no-account husband. He hadn't saved his first lover from her self-destructive ways as a rodeo groupie. He'd meant to do better by Alyssa, thinking he'd spend his life sheltering and protecting her from the unpleasantness of the world, and he'd ended up letting her down, too.

The sun glared off the yellow paper as the woman dangled the flyer between them again. "I was thinking you could put the name of your hotel—"

He pointed at the flyer still snapping in the breeze. "Where did you get that?"

"They have stacks of them in the feed store." She pointed with her thumb. "But, I thought maybe—"

"I know what you thought, darlin', and I'm flattered," he lied. In truth, he'd hardly heard a word she'd said and he didn't give a damn anyway. Let her find some other cowboy's buckle to polish. Or better yet... "Why don't you find some local rancher to take care of you, darlin', and not waste your time chasin' after cowboys who won't be here for you tomorrow?"

Her mouth gaped open in outrage. A sharp gasp expressed her fury with his suggestion.

He shrugged. "Well, do what you will. Like I said, I got unfinished business. Afternoon, ma'am."

With that, he turned on his heel and strode straight into the Feed and Grain to get himself one of the flyers that was going to be the undoing of Miss Alyssa Cartwright.

\* \* \*

*Ka-pow!*

Gold, glittering sparks shimmered in the dusky sky. Alyssa tipped her head up, her lips rounded to join the crowd in one collective "Ooooh."

It had been a great day, a perfect beginning to a terrific new life. She'd given out dozens of business cards and set up meetings with several potential clients. Through it all, she'd been charming, confident and professional, and had still gotten in some quality time with her daughter, who was now on the grandstand with her grandparents enjoying the show.

She shook back her hair, pleased with her new haircut and the way the glossy layers made her feel sassy and sexy for the first time since—

No. She'd promised herself she wasn't going to think about Cub. This whole day had just gone too well for her to start dwelling on past failures, past mistakes.

A shrieking whistle pierced her stomach-clenching thoughts.

High, high up into the ever-darkening sky a rocket soared, casting a radiant yellow light on the upturned heads of the gathered guests. Across that sea of awe-struck faces, someone was not focused on the sizzling light show overhead. Before the fiery blossom fizzled and sent spirals of white vapor plummeting downward, Alyssa caught a glimpse of movement. That one glimpse chilled her to her soul.

A hat, smoked brown, with a cattleman's crown and Aussie brim—she'd swear she saw it. Her pulse thudded in her ears like a string of firecrackers exploding inside a metal drum. She strained to peer into the dimness, into the murmuring mass of people, but saw nothing. Had she imagined it?

She twisted one finger in her hair but the new cut

refused to wind around and only lapped at her circling knuckle. With one deep breath, she squared her shoulders. Exhaling slowly, she patted her hands down her beige linen shortsuit as if needing a physical reminder that this was the new Alyssa Cartwright and she was totally in control.

*Pheee-ueew!* Another rocket whizzed skyward.

You're imagining things, she told herself then trained her gaze on the brilliant red fireworks display. She gritted her teeth to keep from scanning the newly lit crowd once more in search of something logic told her she would not find. She tried to breathe steadily but the very air she dragged into her lungs felt the consistency of muddy water—and about as appealing. She tried to swallow. She tried to keep her eyes on the sky. Tried and failed.

"Aaahhh." The crowd welcomed the next spate of flickering colors.

Alyssa turned and searched desperately for Cub Goodacre's trademark hat with the anticipation of a shipwrecked sailor waiting for the shark's fin to appear.

There. She saw it and then the outline of the wearer. It *was* Cub—and he was headed straight for her. In fact, he looked as if he would reach her any—

The light above faded, putting the whole scene in a blue-black shroud again.

Her pulse hammering, Alyssa turned on the heel of her ballerina flat. She had to get out of here. Yes, she had wanted him to come back, but not like this, just showing up. She needed more time. She needed to prepare herself. She needed to get out of there before he got to her.

"Excuse me," she repeated again and again as she picked her way toward the house and safety.

*Pop. Pop-pop. Pop-pop-pop.*

Alyssa nearly leapt out of her skin with every ear-splitting snap but she forged ahead. On the steps of the huge white house that looked a tacky tribute to Tara, Graceland, God and country, she relaxed enough to take one last glance back at the crowd.

No hat. No circling shark. She blinked.

A fountain of red and blue sparks shot upward, illuminating the view from the ground up.

No Cub Goodacre.

She exhaled and in doing so realized she'd held her breath so long and so hard, her chest actually ached to release it. How could she have let her mind play tricks on her like that?

Fear of failure, clear and simple, she decided. She had had her first taste of success today, known that this time she wasn't going to crash and burn like she had in her last attempt to stand on her own. Then what should leap up and try to scare her into behaving like the old Alyssa? Only the image of her greatest failure as a daughter, a wife, and an independent woman—Cub Goodacre.

The very idea was laughable, really. Cub, here. On her parents' ranch after three years without so much as a "Fare thee well or go to hell."

She forced a chuckle through her dry throat, shook her head and turned to go inside.

*Pshhheeeuw! Boom. Bang. Bang.* A blaze of colors bloomed like enormous flaming parachutes opening against the star-strewn sky, bathing the scene below in a red and yellow glow.

*Pppt…Pppt…Pppt…*

"Hello, Alyssa."

*Pow!*

"Cub!"

Alyssa shut her eyes, half hoping the mirage would fade.

Red shone against her lids with another burst above her. Even so, she could still see the image of a man in faded jeans so perfectly snug they could have grown over his lean thighs and tight calves instead of being bought from a rack. She saw in tantalizing detail the denim shirt, tailored to fit against the rock-hard torso tapering upward to shoulders so broad they made a woman lose herself in sweet dreams of safety and security—and lovemaking as wild as any bull ride.

She could even see the scar that trailed along his jaw to just under his chin. An old rodeo injury had given him that little souvenir, the damage leaving his voice perpetually husky, so that even when he asked someone to pass the sugar, it sounded like an indecent proposal.

She laid her palm across the open V above her breasts. Her skin felt damp. Her head swirled. No mere mirage could make her feel this way.

Slowly, she opened her eyes. He loomed real and dangerously sexy before her. Cub Goodacre was here in the flesh.

Glistening golden and tinged with red light, he stood on her doorstep. He pulled his hat from his head and pushed his long, blunt fingers through his closely cropped black hair. "Looks like a perfect night for a few fireworks, wouldn't you say?"

After three years, he'd hardly changed at all. His body still looked as hard and exquisite as any marble statue, his face rough-hewn as any jagged piece of South Dakota Badlands. The glittering sparks reflected in the depths of his ice-blue eyes, made them seem bottomless and cold—yet lit by some distant incandescent fire.

She didn't need to look long into those eyes to know

that he was angry. Good, she thought, she was angry, too. She had three years of anger and disappointment and pain in her. If he expected to let her have it for what she'd done to him, well, he'd get as good as he gave—and then some.

This wasn't the old Alyssa he was dealing with now. This was Alyssa the strong independent thinker. Alyssa the savvy, charming businesswoman. Alyssa the mother.

Her stomach lurched. Jaycie. She whipped her head around to make sure the baby remained in Yip Cartwright's capable grasp before she turned to Cub again. The best defense is a good offense, she told herself, going on attack.

"You have some nerve showing up here, Goodacre." She planted her hands on her hips, hoping her moist palms would not stain her linen outfit and give her nervousness away. "I'd ask you what you wanted but that might give you the impression I give a damn."

He had no answer for that. Clearly, he hadn't reckoned on meeting up with anything but the docile, doting girl she had once been. He studied her from beneath the sharp angles of his dark eyebrows.

Taking advantage of his hesitation, she decided to make a hasty retreat. Yes, she would have to see him sometime, and she would have to find a way to tell him about their child, but not here, not now. She lunged for the door but as her hand closed over the big brass door handle, Cub closed in on her.

The heat of his body pressed down over her. Her racing heart stilled as a shudder crept up her spine. The fervor of the crowd and the rumblings of the fireworks faded in her ears; her entire world narrowed to just this moment, just this man.

"Whoa there, Alyssa *Cartwright*."

She tensed at the name, his veiled accusation of her betrayal in proclaiming their marriage a fraud. His callused palm closed over the soft skin of her hand, stopping her from opening the door.

"I didn't come out here to be treated to a view of your backside." Cub's chest rose and fell. The scent of her hair, her skin, her nearness filled his lungs and his very being. He held it trapped inside him as he fought to keep his cool exterior. He clenched his jaw and lowered his voice to a rasping, bedroom growl. "Not that I don't thoroughly enjoy the view."

It was no lie. The sight of Alyssa again startled his senses in ways he hadn't thought possible. Her hair, her eyes, her willowy body aged into womanhood with a fullness and rounding like ripe fruit about to burst from its skin, all tempted him. He had no way to prepare himself for the reality of seeing her again, of being so close neither of them could move or even breathe without the other feeling it.

He had no way of preparing himself for the woman he now saw, full of grit and a grace under pressure he hadn't suspected lurked beneath the blushing sweetness of her innocence. A woman who, it seemed, had no other response to him but scorn.

Something primal in him wanted to make her pay for that—not to hurt her, but to put things on equal footing between them.

"Listen, Goodacre." She tossed back her hair, keeping her face forward. "One scream from me and you're off this ranch on the next skyrocket."

"Ain't scared of that," he murmured into the thick warmth of her hair. "I've ridden hotter things. Ridden 'em hard and fast, till I reckoned we'd both of us burn up from the heat and fury."

He heard her pulling in a long, soft gasp and he smiled.

"Remember, Alyssa?"

Her spine went rigid. She turned her profile to him, her voice as dry as sparks when a knife scrapes flint, her words sharpened by her strangled emotion. "I remember, Cub. I also remember thinking I'd nearly drown in my own tears when I realized that for all its fire, that passion had only been a convenient lie."

He should have seen that one coming, but he hadn't. He knew she'd used his going back on the circuit to get herself an annulment—marriage under false pretenses, she said. But until this moment, he hadn't understood that she thought that meant nothing they'd shared had been true or valid. The realization stuck low in his gut and sent searing pain through his entire body. A lie— that's how she summed up what, for him, had been the pivotal experience of his life.

"I...I can't have this discussion with you now," she said.

The pleading in her tone, joined with the stark devastation he felt at learning how the woman who held his heart saw him, made him step back.

A liar. He'd been called worse but it had never sliced into his soul as Alyssa's accusation did.

The lever of the door handle clicked quietly.

Somewhere behind them a band blared to accompany the frenzied finale to the fireworks show.

She pushed the door open. "Call the house tomorrow and maybe we can set up a time to talk."

"No."

"What?" For the first time, she turned to face him.

He forced his gaze to lock with hers. Don't back down now, he told himself. He'd come here for a reason, to purge her from his system or at least ensure she wouldn't be there to jinx his all-important next ride. Despite the pain just standing here caused him, he wasn't about to go with that mission left unaccomplished. "We both know a busted-up bull rider like me ain't good enough to be husband nor lover to a woman like you. No reason to pretend otherwise."

Something flickered in the liquid pools of her hazel eyes. Her gaze denied his words but her lips did not.

He nodded and glanced down at his hat in his hand. "But I won't be dismissed by you Alyssa. Not *this* time."

"I never *dismissed* you."

"No, you just had me annulled."

Her straight white teeth sank into the glistening flesh of her lower lip. He kind of got the notion she wanted to say something, but didn't have the courage.

Guess that meant she did need him, after all; she needed him to keep her from saying something her eyes told him she might regret. "You recall the last words you said to me, darlin'?"

She tilted her chin up but said nothing.

"You said, 'If you can't accept my help to support a ranch, then we aren't partners. If we aren't partners, then in my eyes we aren't married and we never were. From this day out, you are not my husband, Cub Goodacre.'"

Alyssa's gaze never faltered, though her voice did tremble as she said, "And do you recall your last words to me?"

"You know I do," he forced the words hard through his teeth.

"You said you'd come home to me when you'd proved yourself worthy." Moisture shimmered in her eyes but not a single tear fell, as if she willed them not to betray her. "If that's why you're here now, Cub, I have to tell you, too much has happened since you left. It's too late."

That's exactly what he had wanted to hear. Why, then, did it rip at his heart so? His mind unable to settle on any one response, he pressed his fingers to the crown of his hat. The paper tucked inside crackled, drawing him back to his purpose and providing him something to focus on.

"I came because of this, Alyssa." He reached inside the inner brim of his hat and withdrew the yellow paper he'd taken from the feed store. He pushed his hat down on his head, glad to have the brim dipped over his eyes again. He didn't want to accidentally reveal anything to a woman who thought so little of him.

Slowly, he began to unfold the single page.

Alyssa's peaches-and-cream face went pale. She studied the flyer as though she'd never seen it before—or maybe as if she *had* seen it and it somehow contained her greatest secret come back to haunt her.

He gave the flyer one firm shake, playing it up big for her sake. One corner of the page lifted and Cub shook it again to put the picture side to her instead of the blank side.

He shifted his hips, using the pain that movement caused to add substance to his voice when he thrust the photo of his boots in her face and said, "I came because when I saw *this* I realized that you have something that belongs to me."

## Chapter Two

He knows!

Heat flushed her face. The shuffling sounds of departing party-goers filled her ears. Shock stopped her breath cold in the back of her throat.

Her once fondest desire and now greatest fear had both become reality in one ruthless flash of paper. And it was all her own fault. The picture she'd used to launch her new career had accomplished what three years of prayers and tears and searching could not.

Cub knew about their daughter. And now that he knew, everything she'd planned for her own future hung in jeopardy.

A thousand questions flew through her mind, none of them lingering long enough for her to form any clear conclusions. What did Cub want? He'd said no wife of his would work in town; she could only conclude that went double for the mother of his child. Would he fight her for custody now that she had chosen to pursue a career outside the home?

Her eyes darted to the creased picture of the precocious child with so many of Cub's physical attributes and every ounce of his disposition.

Surely, Cub hadn't come here to try to take her child. He wouldn't do that. Her heartbeat slowed to a heavy, thudding knell. Would he?

She raised her chin and concentrated on looking self-confident. "I don't think we should have this discussion without our lawyers present, Cub."

"Lawyers?" The paper crumpled in his fist and he lowered his outstretched arm. "Why the hell would we need lawyers to talk about you giving me my boots back?"

"Boots?"

She batted her lashes, trying to make all the pieces fit. Cub didn't know diddly—at least not about their baby. He'd come here to lay claim to a pair of sorry old sod-kickers, not his one and only flesh-and-blood baby.

Cocking her hip, she cupped one hand to her ear to compound her sarcasm. "Excuse me? But did you say…*boots?*"

"Yeah, boots." He shifted his feet, a quick grimace passing over his features when he did. "Don't try to deny they're mine, Alyssa. The proof is in the picture."

He held the photocopied flyer up again.

Alyssa pretended to skim the page but her gaze quickly fixed past the picture to its real-life subject. Jaycie, riding high on her grandfather's shoulders, giggled and waved a merry "bye-bye" to the thinning crowd. Meanwhile, every stride of Yip Cartwright's long legs brought them closer to a confrontation with disaster.

She did not have a minute to lose. She would tell Cub that she'd never gotten the annulment, that she wanted now to proceed with a divorce. And, of course, she'd tell him about his daughter, even make arrangements for the two of them to meet. Then, somehow, she'd find the strength to deal with the consequences of that meeting. But not now, not under these strained circumstances.

"You're right, Cub, those are your boots." She edged sideways drawing his gaze like enemy gunfire, away from her approaching child. "I'm sorry I used them without your permission, but it isn't exactly like I could have gotten your permission if I had wanted it, now could I?"

"Well…"

"I mean, it isn't like you wouldn't have just sent my letter back unopened, right?" She took another sidelong step, keenly aware that her father and her daughter were getting closer by the second. "You sent back every letter that ever reached you."

He glared at her, huffing hard through his nostrils as his lean cheek ticked in tightly reined anger.

Good, she thought. She might not have known Cub well enough to make a life with him, but she did know this: if she made it clear enough that she did not want him here, he'd go.

"I can't believe that after all this time, you'd come way out here to pick and quibble over some beat-up old boots, anyway, Cub." The night breeze lifted the layers of her hair as she spun on her heel and marched down the side steps of the brick porch. "It's just too ridiculous. Why don't I walk you to your truck and we can set a better time to talk?"

He did not follow her lead.

Her neck cramped as she twisted her head to cast a frosty look over her shoulder. "You did drive out in a truck, didn't you? I don't recall seeing a twin suspension, four-hoof-drive bull parked out—"

"The only bull around here, Alyssa, darlin', is what's pouring out of those pretty little lips of yours." He planted his big boots at the top of the stairs and folded his arms over the fresh cotton of his shirt.

"Me?" She cursed the squeak of surprise in her forced response but thanked her lucky stars that was all that her voice betrayed.

One more long look at Cub, from the set of his custom-made hat down the length of his bull rider's body, filled her with far more than astonishment. "I don't know whether to be flattered that you think I'm suddenly so sly that I'd dare to match wits with an old bull artist like yourself or just angry at the fact that you won't respect my wishes and let me walk you—"

"I ain't a dog that needs walking anywhere, Alyssa." Cub's shirt rustled as he shifted his expansive shoulders.

Jaycie's laughter drifted above the clatter of lawn chairs and the murmuring crowd.

Alyssa faced Cub, taking a step backward in hopes of coaxing him to follow.

"What I think," she said, taking yet another small step, "is that this is neither the time nor place for us to talk."

His lips twitched but he said nothing.

"Let's get this little one to bed, Ma," Alyssa heard Yip tell her mother, Dolly.

Drastic situations called for drastic measures, she thought. If she truly was a new woman, strong enough to stand on her own without Cub Goodacre, then she surely could be strong enough to stand up *to* him. "I'm not trying to walk you like a dog, Cub, but if you don't stop being so stubborn about leaving, I may just grab you by your collar and *run* you off my ranch."

The thin scar along his deeply tanned jaw and neck

shown pinkish red in the moonlight as he tipped his head to one side. He didn't smile, but amusement tinged his tone when he ran one finger along the side of his thick neck and said in a gruff whisper, "Is that so?"

Despite her anxiety, she couldn't help noticing how his dark skin contrasted against the crisp whiteness of his stiff collar. Or how his sandpaper-and-velvet voice massaged her prickling nerves like warm fingertips over aching muscles.

"That's so." The answer lacked the conviction she'd hoped for but it got her message across. She wasn't the guileless child he'd once known. She was the woman in charge.

Just over Cub's shoulder, Alyssa watched Yip pause to strike up a conversation with someone just a few feet from the porch. Nothing she had tried worked, and any second now her father would move right behind Cub. Perhaps sooner, her daughter would see her and call out. She had to find another way to get Cub to leave before that happened.

"And now I suggest, Cub, that you—" Somewhere in the crowd, she heard her name.

Shelby Crowder, her new business partner, held up one hand to her.

"Who's that?"

It interested Alyssa that she still had enough innocent dreamer left in her to convince herself she heard jealousy in Cub's quiet question.

"That's my…" She paused to lick her lips. Even beneath the cover of his hat brim, she saw a glimmer of an old familiar emotion in his eyes. He *was* jealous.

A flash fire of feelings singed her cheeks.

Cub's face told her he saw her response.

"Your what?" he asked in a husky bass.

Don't blow this, she told herself. Tomorrow when she was calm and prepared, she'd straighten everything out, until then...

"That's Shelby Crowder." She turned to wave back at the handsome red-haired man in the impeccable designer western clothes. When she faced Cub again, she'd puffed her confidence up to meet the enormity of the situation.

Smiling broadly, she told the only lover she'd ever had, the father of her beloved child, the only man who could turn her to jelly with a glance, the one thing that would get him off the ranch in a huff and a hurry. "He's the man I'm going to marry."

Alyssa had fallen in love with another man.

Cub dipped his hands into the cool water pooled in the gold-veined sink in his hotel bathroom. Streams of clear liquid slid between his fingers to trickle back into the sink as he lifted his cupped palms.

He swallowed a gasp as the cold water stung his face and icy droplets splashed onto his bare chest. But when he raised his gaze to confront the man in the mirror, he knew that nothing could wash away the grim reality etched in his features. Alyssa would become some other man's wife and he would wear the pain of losing her for the rest of his life.

He snapped the hand towel from the rack, closing his eyes against the blinding whiteness of the morning sun gleaming on the white-tiled room. As he scrubbed the rough terry cloth over his face, the picture of Shelby Crowder haunted him.

Successful, handsome, well-educated, the solid type—everything Cub was not. Oh, Cub was solid, he supposed, solid with rock-hard muscles and a head to match. As for higher education? He had a couple advanced degrees by now from the school of hard knocks. He'd never been handsome and a few falls facedown in the dirt and one real good slam into an iron gate hadn't prettied him up any.

Still, he'd always thought if he'd worked hard enough and achieved enough he could overcome those obstacles. He'd once believed that if he could earn enough to buy a little spread and take care of Alyssa comfortably he'd prove himself worthy of her love.

Today, because of his hard work and the fact that bull riding meant big money, he'd earned a tidy nest egg and then some. With bull riding's corporate sponsorship, like tennis or NASCAR racing, these days a name rider drew six figures a year. And Cub wasn't just a name rider, he was *the* name rider. He'd met that goal and then some.

And yet, Alyssa was marrying someone else and threatening to run him off her ranch, not even willing to speak to him without an appointment.

He threw the towel across the room.

Every muscle from his neck to his belly clenched as he fought back a wave of regret. Last night when she told him she was marrying again, he'd have given every damned dime he'd ever earned to go back to the last morning he'd woken up with that woman in his arms.

"And do what?" he asked the steam-blurred image in the mirror. The heel of his hand squawked against the glass as he swiped away a circle to see himself clearly.

He would still have left—to earn the money needed to buy a ranch. But this time, he'd wake his wife up to explain it all to her, to make her understand. He hadn't done it the first time because he knew she'd be mad at him for breaking his promise. His life experiences had taught him that anger meant hatred, disgust, rejection.

He hadn't thought he could survive getting those things from Alyssa.

Besides, as the husband, wasn't it his place to make the decisions? To do what he thought best for Alyssa? Her notion of getting a job in a local diner to pay the bills was an affront to his manhood—it was saying outright that he couldn't take care of his own. He'd already been down that road in his life and he wasn't going there again. So starting an argument about something he would take no argument over was just senseless.

And as soon as he'd left, her parents had rushed in to verify what she'd probably suspected all along—she'd made the biggest mistake of her life by putting her faith in him. Poor kid. His actions and the confirmation of her own parents had made her feel a total fool and a failure.

He dragged one knuckle over his freshly shaved cheek. They'd probably both be better off if he hopped in his truck and drove away right now, just forgot about Summit City Rodeo Days and the bull he'd come to do battle with.

He hadn't protected her from unhappiness then, hadn't been the man she needed him to be, beat-up as he was inside and out. He wasn't any better now—worse, if you counted only the physical toll his profession had taken on him. No amount of money he made would change that fact.

But he wasn't riding for money these days; he was riding for his own brand of honor—to go out on top and have something he didn't walk away from when it didn't want him anymore. And he was under contract to make those rides as part of a much publicized duel, five rides to see who was better, man or beast, scheduled almost a full year ago by a high-dollar sponsor. To walk away would mean financial ruin and public humiliation.

His future hung in the balance against those two rides. Alyssa Cartwright wasn't going to take that away from him, too.

He dressed quickly and, just before he walked out the door, donned his trademark hat, pushing it down low over his eyes.

The hotel lobby bustled with rodeo people and the usual hangers-on. More than one lady with faded makeup from the night before and a look of rumpled satisfaction about her smiled at him. He nodded to them but did nothing to encourage any hopeful "buckle bunny" as they sometimes called the rodeo groupies. Despite that, one big-haired gal with gilded boots, leopard-skin fringe on her denim jacket and short skirt dashed up to him, her arms open wide.

He dodged left and what was surely meant as a big wet kiss on the lips glanced off his cheekbone.

"Excuse me, ma'am," he muttered, disguising a quick duck of his head as a nod.

"I can't believe it. I *kissed* Cub Goodacre," the woman cried to a gaggle of similarly dressed gals, who all hooted and high-fived her like teenaged boys in a locker room.

"It's the hat."

"What?" Cub jerked his head up only to find himself face-to-face with Alyssa's fiancé.

"Your hat." The man gestured with one finger toward his own bare head. "It's a stroke of genius."

"It is?" Obviously, he thought, narrowing one eye at the fellow who looked as if he'd just stepped out of some slick western-wear catalogue instead of off the range, Alyssa had snagged herself a loon.

"Of course it is, man." He chuckled as if they were old pals sharing an inside joke. "Why, you walk into a room and everyone knows at a glance that Cub Goodacre has arrived. Heads turn, folks whisper.''

''Like to think that has something to do with my accomplishments, not my headgear.'' He threw back his shoulders to give himself height. This man of Alyssa's stood an inch or so over him and that didn't make Cub like him one bit better.

''Your skill on the bulls is legendary, Cub…can I call you Cub?'' He smiled.

Cub figured if a rattler could smile, that would be just about what it would look like.

''Great, Cub,'' the man went on, seemingly taking Cub's lack of any response as overture to everlasting friendship. ''Now, as I said, your skills speak for themselves and that hat and the strong, silent cowpoke persona you've cultivated, well, they speak for your professional image.''

Cub didn't like this fellow. Did not like him at all.

''But let me ask you this, Cub, who speaks for *you?*''

''I speak for myself.'' Cub flicked his hat up off his face with one sharp pop of his thumb and forefinger. ''May not come out as gussied up and *slick* as your words, mister, but I've done fine so far.''

''Have you, Cub? Have you really?''

The false concern rang like a rusted cowbell in Cub's ears.

''Do you realize,'' the man rushed on, ''that with your reputation and talent you are one hot property?''

How could Alyssa have fallen for this two-bit hustler? Something was not right about this. Still, Cub reminded himself, it wasn't his place any longer to protect Alyssa from foolish choices. That was this fellow's lookout now.

The man narrowed his eyes in presumed familiarity.

"You know, my friend, if you would just capitalize more on your current celebrity, you could be a very wealthy man."

Cub shook his head and started to walk on. "I do all right just as I am."

The man stepped back to keep himself directly in Cub's path.

"Oh, I'm well aware of your considerable winnings these past few years."

"You are?" Cub stopped.

"Got the stats from the National Rodeo Riders Association and frankly, Cub, you are underutilizing your earning potential."

"I am?" He didn't want to listen but the weasel had him hooked.

"Let me tell you, with the proper management to get you endorsements, better sponsorship, maybe a spot in a country music video, next season, you could be pulling down at least twice what you made last year."

"Next season?" Cub huffed out a humorless laugh at the notion. "I'm sorry, buddy, but—"

"Crowder." He thrust his right hand out. "Shelby Crowder."

Cub eyed the man's offered hand. He didn't want to accept the gesture but his lifelong cowboy way of doing things wouldn't let him slight a man he held no founded grudge against. When his palm met Crowder's he gripped it tighter than the reins on a ton of loco bucking bull.

To his credit, Crowder didn't wince. He did ease out a little sigh of relief when Cub turned him loose, though. Then he dove right back into business. "Look, there's no use beating around the bush, Cub. I'm fully aware of your past relationship with Alyssa and I want you to know…''

''Shelby? Cub?'' Alyssa's voice carried across the bustling lobby.

Both men paused and turned toward her. The sight put a rock in Cub's belly. She was still as beautiful in the morning light as she had been three years ago. It wasn't lost on Cub, though, that this morning her easy smile and the flush of her cheeks was for the man standing beside him, not for Cub. He stole a glance at Crowder from the corner of his eye.

Head bowed, the other man seemed far more intrigued by his pager than the woman approaching them. Weasel-boy sure was taking this whole awkward situation lightly, Cub decided. If the roles were reversed and Crowder were the ex-husband, a stampede wouldn't draw Cub's eye from Alyssa. Something was not right about this at all.

He let his gaze swing from Crowder's nonchalant attitude to the overly sweet, yet almost panicked expression on Alyssa's face. Something felt definitely crooked about this relationship and Cub figured he knew a way to bring the truth to light.

''What in mercy's sakes is going on here?'' Whatever it was, Alyssa surmised in a heartbeat, it wasn't likely to be good for her.

Last night, she'd sent Cub on his way before he could meet Shelby and discover her lie. She hadn't even mentioned the wild story to Shelby because the whole thing was so embarrassing. Besides, she had intended to clear it all up when she spoke to Cub later today. Of course, she thought that would be *much* later today.

She stopped beside the two men waiting for her in the practical elegance of the hotel lobby.

Somehow, she'd always pictured Cub staying in cheap out-of-the-way motels, or perhaps even sleeping in his truck as he went from rodeo to rodeo. The lonely, desolate drifter stereotype certainly suited her image of him much better than thinking of him staying in the best hotels, the places swarming with buckle chasing beauties. She should have at least considered, she scolded herself, that a rider as successful as Cub would be at this hotel, where she and Shelby were meeting potential clients this morning.

"Have you two been chatting long?" she asked, gripping her spanking new briefcase over her western cut jacket. She hoped neither of them could hear that rapid thrumming of her heart hammering against the faux alligator case.

"Actually—" Cub very gently placed the point of his boot on top of her shoe, stopping the feverish tapping toe of her pump. "Your... friend, here, has been trying to sell me your management services."

"My management services?" She blinked, struggling to imagine what Shelby had in mind, while her real attention drifted downward to the place where Cub's foot touched hers. Such a simple thing and yet it sent a tingling heat surging upward through her body, making it difficult to concentrate on the conversation.

"*Our* management services," Shelby corrected. "A client like Cub Goodacre could provide the kind of financial anchor we need for our business to stay the long course."

"A client? Cub?" She clutched the case like a life preserver and gave a breathy laugh that didn't fool a soul. "I'm sure he wouldn't be interested in a small-potatoes management firm like ours. Would you, Cub?"

"Gee, I don't know." He stroked his chin, his eyes

downcast as though he were truly considering it. "I was always partial to potatoes."

Not funny, she warned with a glance, sensing he was up to something.

He lifted the toe of his boot from her pump, situating it so that the sides of their legs kept in contact.

Her entire body stiffened but she did not move away from the warmth of his nearness. "What I meant was, I don't think we're ready to handle Cub."

His gaze met hers from under the shadow of his hat. He cocked one eyebrow and his mouth lifted on one side. "I don't know, Alyssa, I can't think of anyone else I'd rather have *handling* me."

She wet her lips. Her fingers caressed the smooth, textured surfaced of her briefcase. "I'm...we're not prepared for that, Cub. You're just...too big."

"And that's a bad thing?"

His husky growl rattled down her spine and created tremors low in her body.

The images and sense memories ambushed her from every direction. The musky scent of their shared bed. The golden light of the sunset streaming on their naked bodies that first time. The insatiable aching deep within her that only the hard, rhythmic power of this one man could ever slake.

A film of sweat dampened the back of her neck; her eyes could not quite focus on anything but Cub's face, Cub's incredible body. She swallowed and brushed her hair back with one limp hand.

"It's...it's not...bad," she murmured. "Not *bad*. But—"

"Are you kidding? It's terrific!" Shelby reached out to slap Cub on the back, but one cutting glare from under that hat brim made the taller man pause mid-gesture and settle for a light jab in the air. "It's terrific. Does this mean you'll consider signing with Crowder and Cartwright?"

"Hell, no." It came more as a chuckle than a curse or an outright rejection.

"No?" Shelby ran one hand back through the waves of his dark red hair. "But can't you see the advantages of—"

"Don't push this, Shelby," Alyssa whispered, hissing out every *s* through clenched teeth. "The man said no and that's it."

The look on Cub's face told her that her new assertiveness took him by surprise. And she felt surprise in return that he did not seem put off by the change in her.

Buoyed by the moment of quiet personal triumph, she angled her chin up and straightened her arm to put her briefcase at her side. "We have clients to meet, Shelby."

"Yeah, I suppose we do," Shelby muttered. Giving Cub a terse nod, he added, "Nice to meet you, Goodacre. If you should have a change of heart—"

"Alyssa will be the first to know," Cub finished for him.

"I'll talk to *you* later," she told Cub, hoping the air of aloofness would keep him from seeking her out before she was ready to deal with him.

"Guess you will, " he replied. "Providing I ain't too *big* to talk to you."

She narrowed her eyes at him and contemplated some scathing remark but the sharp, steady beeping of Shelby's pager intruded.

"Good gosh, Alyssa, this is *it*." Shelby spun on his heel and almost ran straight over her in his rush to get to the hotel door.

"Are you sure?" she asked, stopping his flight with

an upheld hand. "Remember last time, it was just a desperate plea for Chinese food."

"Oh, I'm sure all right. I mean she *is* eight days overdue already and—" He checked the beeper clipped to his belt, then put his hands on Alyssa's shoulders to gently move her aside. "I can't have this discussion now, Alyssa. I have to go."

"But what about our meetings?" she asked her partner's back.

"You can handle the meetings. I have complete faith in your abilities." He reached for the silver bar handle on the swinging door.

"But what if I mess up?" Panic strangled her voice.

"You won't."

"But what if—"

"You won't. You'll do fine." He shoved open the door and glanced back, a great, big, goofy grin on his handsome face. "*I'm* the one should be worried, partner. After all, it's my wife about to have our first baby."

A whoosh of air and Shelby was gone.

Alyssa's fingers wound around the briefcase handle until her nails dug into her palm and her knuckles throbbed. What was she supposed to do now? Could she really get out there and pitch the business all by herself?

A wave of nausea hit her, her stomach churned like boiling oil and her skin grew cool and clammy. She did not want all this responsibility to rest on her shoulders just yet. She wasn't ready and if she failed…

A big hand clamped down on her shoulder, disrupting her misgivings and misery.

Cub. He'd heard the whole exchange. Just when she thought things could not get any more complicated or any more difficulties crop up between her and her dream of independence, the man gently turned her to face him.

His eyes grave, he placed one hand under her quivering chin and raised her face so that their gazes locked.

"Let me get this straight, Alyssa." His brow creased with obvious concern. "Your fiancé can't make your business appointments today because his *wife* is having a baby?"

"Much as I'd love to stand here and tell you just how truly twisted up I've gotten my life, Cub, I don't have the time." She pushed past him, unable to meet his damning glare. "You'll just have to wait until you come out to the ranch this afternoon and I can make a clean breast of everything."

# *Chapter Three*

Cub jabbed his finger into the pearly center of the Cartwrights' ornate doorbell.

The harsh electric buzzer pricked at his already raw nerves. Scraps of paper, remnants of last night's festivities, swirled over the porch behind him. A yellow flyer like the ones he had seen yesterday snagged on a huge decorative planter and began to rattle in the wind. That noise didn't help to calm him.

He craned his neck, then worked back his shoulder trying to ease out the tension gripping his muscles. Using the rolled back cuff of his shirtsleeve, he rubbed his forearm over his latest championship belt buckle. The sun glinted off the brilliant gold and silver, stinging his eyes.

He brushed the top of his boot down the length of his calf to wipe away any fresh dust. When he lifted his second boot to do the same, white-hot ripping pain shot through his body.

The doctor would slap Cub's sorry butt right back in

physical therapy if the man had any idea what kind of stress this battered hip had taken these last few days. Staying too long on his feet, walking all over town and never using a cane all broke the strict rules given him by one of the top sports-medicine physicians in the country. According to that doctor, Cub could count himself lucky if he could manage to make these last two career-crowning rides without doing so much damage he would require a total hip replacement. And that Shelby Crowder weasel had talked of plans for *next* season.

Cub huffed. The thought of Crowder took his mind off his physical problems and focused it on trouble of another kind.

Alyssa. What was that girl up to? And why on earth had she found it necessary to lie about being engaged to her business partner? It was a lie, Cub felt sure of it.

He'd seen the changes in Alyssa. Seen right off the air of confidence, her new spunk, the spark in her eyes that had not been there three years ago. Despite all that, he knew the girl could not have changed so much she'd be capable of the kind of duplicity it took to get involved with a married man.

One of the things that had attracted him to Alyssa had been her trusting nature and unyielding honesty. Because of those traits he had known that when she said she loved him that she meant it—just as he'd known that when she told him the trust between them was broken she meant that, too. No matter what part her parents might have played in her getting the annulment, Cub knew that Alyssa would not have done it if her heart had not been in it.

He'd returned her letters unopened for that very reason. He needed no further explanation for her actions. If they had gotten back together they would have lived each day waiting for the other shoe to drop. Alyssa would be watching for him to slip up so she could confirm to herself—and her family—that her judgment could not be trusted. Cub, on the other hand, would bide his time, knowing that any day he would fall short of her needs and expectations.

The women he'd loved had never been able to count on him.

And so he did what he had to do—moved on without her, making it clear by not allowing any contact with her that the relationship they had once known had been forever severed.

The relationship was gone but his feelings for her remained. They always would, he thought, his heart heavy with a familiar ache. Unless, he added silently, she *had* actually changed so much that she could take up with another woman's husband. Then, he could let go of the Alyssa he had once loved and sacrificed himself for, because she no longer existed.

He shook his head, not able to believe that of Alyssa.

The wind picked up, whipping the debris in a circle and freeing the yellow flyer from the planter. He caught a glimpse of delicate handwriting on the back as the torn paper went gliding past the tips of his boots.

Curious, he bent to retrieve it but before he could read a single word, the door swung open. He jerked his head up, his fingers folding the flyer in quarters without thinking any more about it.

Alyssa stood in the doorway, her eyes following his actions with more interest than was warranted.

Cub stuffed the folded paper into his back pocket and that seemed to break the hold the flyer had on Alyssa.

"Sorry I took so long to get to the door," she said,

her face flushed. "I was putting the...well, it's all right now."

At the sight of her, Cub forgot all about the paper. He had better things to focus on than some ratty note.

"Hello, Alyssa," he murmured, straightening his body.

Seeing her like this, not in some polished outfit but in faded jeans and a white T-shirt, took him aback. For all his brave talk about letting go of her, one face-to-face moment and his mind and body had filled with one primal urge—to take her in his arms.

Did she still feel the powerful pull between them? Would she reject him if he reached for her?

"Hello...Cub." Her sweet, pink lips closed over his name, then came apart again as if she wanted to say more—or perhaps be kissed.

He made a quick study of her to determine which.

Strawberry-blond hair in tousled layers feathered against her cheeks and neck. Her chest rose and fell in shallow breaths. She smelled of lavender and baby powder.

This is how she looks after a long, leisurely session of lovemaking, he thought. A rolling ball of sexual energy roared southward through his body. If he leaned in, he could put his mouth over hers and—

"Well, don't just loiter around on the porch." Her tone said kissing was not in order. She stepped aside to indicate he should enter the house.

He swept his hat from his head, holding it in both hands to conceal the evidence of her effect on him, and stepped inside.

"Let's talk in the front room," Alyssa said as she led the way, her back as stiff as her tone. "Mama and Daddy are in town for the afternoon so we don't have to worry over them spoiling our privacy."

Alone with Alyssa. How long had he dreamt of this very thing? His gaze drifted to her denim-cupped, round behind and the sight stirred all the old longings to a new high.

She peered at him over her shoulder as she walked through the foyer. "Can I take your hat?"

He glanced down at his bulging jeans. "Um, I think I'll keep it with me, thanks."

She nodded.

In the front room, with its tall windows and Italian tile fireplace, she motioned for him to take a seat on the carved cherry-wood settee.

He perched on the edge of the striped velvet cushion, feeling more like a blundering bull than a skilled bull rider among the fine things. Leaning both forearms on his thighs, he kept his gaze fixed on Alyssa as her hand pulled aside one voluminous sheer curtain. Sunlight poured in to outline her shoulders and the curve of her silhouette.

Cub blamed some trick of the light and his own raging desire for the fact that her breasts appeared larger than he remembered them, her hips fuller in contrast to her slender waist.

She let the curtain fall, then turned slowly to face him.

Cub swallowed hard, his hat still in his hands.

She flicked one finger through the hair tumbling against her neck. Her tongue tipped out to wet her lips. She inhaled, her breasts thrusting upward. Her voice rushed out, hushed and intimate with her breath. "Um, before we start, can I get you anything?"

He jerked his head up to meet her gaze, his own breath stopped like a stone in his throat.

"Something cold, perhaps?" she asked.

How about a shower? he thought. Get a grip on yourself, his common sense finally horned in to warn him. He cleared his throat and shook his head. "Nothing, thanks. What I really want is an explanation about this Crowder fellow."

She pulled her shoulders up. "I don't owe you any explanations concerning my personal life, Cub Goodacre. You lost the right to that kind of thing three years ago."

The hard-hearted witch routine fit her about as well as his boots fit that baby wrangler in her flyer. Still, it stung something fierce to hear her speak to him in that way.

"I realize you don't owe me anything, Alyssa," he whispered, intending to say something more, but she cut him off.

"That's not true, Cub." Her more natural softness returned. "I owe you a lot more than you can understand at the moment. But for now, let me start with an apology."

"An apology?" He inched forward on the cushion. "For what?"

She crossed her arms. Her gaze dipped downward. "I lied. Shelby Crowder isn't anything to me but my business partner."

"No kidding," he deadpanned.

"You knew?"

"I'm a bull rider because I'm good at it, darlin', not because I'm too dense to do anything else." A brittle tension hung between them. His sarcasm did nothing to ease it.

Still, Alyssa managed a cynical grin and a chuckle. "I never called you stupid, Cub, but I wouldn't call you subtle either. If I'm surprised it's not that you knew but that you didn't call me out on it straightaway.''

"You got me there," he said.

*Got him?* Even a few days ago the very notion would have made her giddy with the possibilities, but now, faced with the reality that Cub was sitting in her home made her almost soul-sick. Alyssa blinked and straightened, letting the joking façade fall away. It had only been a diversion, a stalling tactic to lighten the air before she made her serious, potentially life-altering confession.

"Cub, I have changed…and, well, my life has changed," she said, moving to lean against the doily-covered arm of the chair across from where he sat.

"I can see that, Alyssa. You look different and you act it." He laid his hat down on the settee next to him. "More…in control."

"Thank you." She couldn't look at him. Her attention went to the window and the glaring sunlight brought soothing dampness to her dry eyes. "But there are other changes, ones that don't show."

His gaze burned on her face like sun magnified through a looking glass, but she could not make herself meet it.

Long into the night, she had practiced ways of revealing her secret to this man she loved but could never make a life with. She rubbed her knuckle in the corner of her eye, buying herself a moment to allow the groundswell of old pain to subside. When she told Cub the truth, she would do it without tears or regrets. She would show him exactly how much she had changed, how much "in control" she really was. She would face him as the woman she knew herself to be, not the girl he expected.

She focused on the curtains, the fireplace, the throw

rug, then finally on the pair of black snakeskin boots standing in the corner of the room. "Cub? You know that flyer you had—the one with the picture of a baby wearing your cowboy boots?"

His gaze followed hers. "Hey, my boots."

He rose slowly from the settee, and Alyssa almost thought she heard him squeeze off a cussword through his teeth when he did.

She narrowed her eyes to watch him walk stiffly across the room, as if his leg had fallen asleep.

He stopped beside the boots, took a deep breath, then bent at the knees, lowering his body inch by inch until he could reach out to stroke the weathered leather upper.

Despite her building anxiety, Alyssa watched, mesmerized, as Cub's strong, blunt fingers curved over the textured snakeskin of the boot toe. Those hands had once caressed her skin with a tenderness so rare that even its memory made her tremble.

"It's been a long time," Cub said in that rough, husky whisper of his.

"It certainly has." She rubbed one open palm over the prickling goosebumps on her bare arm. "A long time."

He raised his head at her words and turned his profile to her.

Had he heard the naked longing in her voice? Alyssa touched her fingertips to her lips and waited for his response.

Cub picked up the boots with one hand, then stood. When he did, his leg wobbled, ever so slightly. His tanned jaw clenched, making the scar there more pronounced. The crisp cotton of his shirt furrowed between his shoulder blades as his muscular back rippled.

"These boots saw me through a lot of good times—

even wore them the night we eloped.'' He said it like a man testing the waters.

"I...I remember." Alyssa gripped the back of the chair until her fingers went almost numb. If Cub suspected she had any feelings left for him, she was a goner. *A goner.*

Armed with that knowledge and the fact that they had a child together, he might push for a reconciliation. Feeling as she did now, her heart and body humming with the benevolent torment of his nearness, she would go to him. And he would—without meaning to—destroy the courage and self-reliance she had taken so long to rebuild in herself.

That cold reality steeled Alyssa's will. She had no future with a man like Cub, a man who thought his role was to shelter and protect her. If he could see her as an equal, as the assertive, intelligent woman she had worked hard to become, then...

Then, nothing. That would never happen, and dreaming about it would only cause pain and misery for both of them. She released her death grip on the chair and flipped her hair off her shoulder. "But I didn't ask you here to talk about the boots, Cub—or the past."

Cub sighed, then ran his free hand back through his jet-black hair. "I figured it wasn't the boots."

He turned, his entire body stiff, tightly controlled. Something flashed in his blue eyes, then faded.

She gulped back the bitter fear coursing through her body and tipped her chin up. She was just going to say it outright. Her lips quivered, but parted. She drew a breath so deep it hurt all the way to her rigid backbone.

"So, Alyssa," he said, in his rasping, soft way. "If you don't want to hash out our past, then what did you want to talk to me about?"

"Mine!"

Jaycie burst through the arched doorway to the front room, her pudgy bare feet slapping against the hard floor as she thundered to the rescue of her prized boots.

Alyssa gasped and took one step toward the child, who was supposed to be safely tucked away napping. Her heartbeats were like hammer blows on an anvil as she tried to snag her daughter, but Jaycie dodged her attempt. Humiliation and horror washed over her, followed by an odd sense of peace that her secret was finally out—out and squealing like an angry piglet.

"My boots. Mine!" Jaycie's small fingers wriggled to grasp the cowboy boots dangling just out of her reach.

Cub gaped at the small girl wearing a faded blue T-shirt and plastic training pants sagging low on her plump behind. When his gaze moved from the child to Alyssa, he looked as stunned as if he'd been kicked in the head by a bull.

*Just say it outright.* Her decision of a moment earlier haunted her. Show Cub you *are* in control, her gut instincts added, even when the world around you is chaos.

With that thought planted squarely in her mind, she stepped forward and lifted Jaycie up. The baby squirmed against her, her pale red hair rubbing Alyssa's burning cheek.

Kicking, Jaycie howled out her demands in her limited vocabulary. "Down. Want down. *My* boots. Mine!"

Above the din, Alyssa lifted her head, met Cub's gaze head-on and said, "*This* is what I need to talk to you about. Congratulations, Cub Goodacre, you are a father."

# Chapter Four

Every square inch of his body and all but one corner of his mind went numb. That one coherent bit of brain matter told him this just wasn't happening. It could not be true. He did not *want* this to be true.

He didn't know the first thing about children except for his own firsthand experience of how much a parent could screw a child up. He wanted no part of doing that to another human being. He was a cowboy, damn it, that's all he was good for. No way could he be a—

He lifted his head and narrowed his eyes at Alyssa for confirmation. "A what?"

"A father," Alyssa repeated, struggling to maintain control of the child in her arms.

"Down! My boots." The plump toddler strained each of her pudgy fingers toward the boots in his white-knuckled grasp.

His gaze riveted to the squalling scrap of red hair and determination with Alyssa's eyes and *his* stubborn streak. "You mean this...this...this is—"

"Mine!"

"Yours." Alyssa curved her hand gently over the child's head.

A joy like none he'd ever known rose to mingle with a pain and apprehension so fierce it only registered as heat and heaviness in his chest. His throat closed. Despite the sudden stirrings of parental emotion, something in him shuddered. A life-scarred loner like him had no business being a father.

His eyes burned and without knowing how or why, soothing dampness followed. He blinked and the moisture cleared, but his already ragged voice sounded strained and so quiet, he feared Alyssa would not hear when he asked, "Why didn't you tell me?"

"I did." She lowered the child to the floor but did not relinquish her hold. "Letter after letter came back unopened. You never seemed to stay in any one place long enough for me to reach you by phone, and I was in no condition to hop in a truck and chase you down on the rodeo circuit."

His gaze fell to her now flat belly and the significance of her whole situation hit him like a wave. She'd carried his child alone, given birth alone, cared for their baby alone. If he thought he'd let her down before, that was nothing compared to mess he'd made of this.

He hung his head. "Alyssa, I—"

"Mine! My boots."

A stiff little yank jiggled the boots in his hand. The child had broken away from Alyssa and lunged for the prize she had demanded.

Alyssa gasped softly.

Cub let his gaze fall to the headstrong imp trying to engage him in a tug-of-war. For the first time in his life,

Cub gazed into the eyes of his very own child. The intensity of the connection he felt took his breath away.

"Mine." His lips formed the word his mind could not yet quite fully comprehend.

"Jaycie, no." Alyssa stepped forward.

He jerked his head up. "J.C.? Jacob Christopher? You named him after me?"

"J-A-Y-C-I-E, it's a nickname, short for Jayne Cartwright." Alyssa folded her arms over her chest. "I named *her* after my grandmother—you know, one of the West's original cow*girls?*"

"Her? A girl?" It figured he'd father a girl, didn't it?

His lousy track record with females and somehow the Lord Almighty had seen fit to give him one of his very own, one who, after just a moment of looking in her eyes, Cub wanted to hear her call him Daddy—and to deserve the title. If he hadn't already started off his daughter's life by letting her down, he'd think it was all a pretty slick joke.

Trying to force some humor in his tone, he muttered, "You had to go and have a girl."

"Don't say it like I did it out of spite for you." Alyssa reached for Jaycie.

"No," the little one squealed at her mother's touch. "My boots."

Cub's gaze fell to his once treasured boots, then to the child he felt totally unprepared to deal with.

"No. No, no, no." Jaycie's round face went stern.

"She sure is familiar with that word," he murmured, his gaze now fixed on the strong-willed tot.

"It's part of being two." Alyssa scooped the child up again.

Now they stood so close to him, he could feel the swing of Jaycie's pink foot against Alyssa's arm, see the tension around Alyssa's eyes and the pale color of her full lips.

"So, she's two." Two. A short measure by most standards but his child's entire life. Guilt burrowed deep into his chest and throbbed with every dull heartbeat. What more proof did he need that he wasn't meant to be a father?

"No." Jaycie pushed her lower lip out and shook her finger in warning at him. "My boots. Give to the baby."

"The baby?" He arched an eyebrow at the strange reference.

"She's *two*," Alyssa said as if that explained everything. "At two, they don't have an individual identity yet."

"She seems to have identity to spare, darlin'." That meant his child was advanced for her age, he decided, feeling his chest puff with fatherly pride despite his anxiety about the role.

"Identity is an outgrowth of maturity, Cub. Don't confuse a strong personality with maturity." She tossed back her hair and then dropped her gaze to his with deadly aim. "It's an easy mistake to make."

"Ouch." He chuckled. A challenge to his maturity didn't threaten his masculinity one bit. He'd been born an adult, he'd had to be to survive. If anyone had lacked maturity in their relationship, it was Alyssa. Still, if it gave her comfort to think otherwise, what did it hurt him? He owed her every shred of confidence that belief offered and then some.

She cradled the wriggling toddler with a firmness that seemed unrelenting to the child's protests and yet very maternal. "Jaycie is in a developmental stage where she's just beginning to separate herself from her surroundings, to learn who she is. Sometimes they call it the 'terrible twos.'"

Cub nodded, still feeling stunned. What he didn't know about babies could fill a bookshelf—and it could go right above the bookshelf filled with what he didn't know about women.

He blinked at the mother of his child. He'd once worried she couldn't handle the basic tasks of daily life, a job, a home, making financial decisions—and that she needed to depend on him for those things. But when faced with the greatest challenge of her abilities, she'd met and surpassed his expectations. He wondered now if he had ever really known Alyssa at all. He certainly didn't know this woman. But he wished with all his heart to have a chance to get to know her, and their child.

"Mama! My boots." Jaycie grunted in pure frustration.

Alyssa hoisted the unhappy child up high against her chest. "Sorry about this, but she's kind of attached to the boots."

"I guessed."

"No, Jaycie, these are *his* boots. They belong to *him*."

"Him bad." Jaycie pointed her finger at Cub.

So that's all he was, not Daddy, not someone Alyssa had told their child about. *Him.*

"Him take from the baby."

A gash from a rusty blade wouldn't have hurt like that did.

"No, darlin'." Cub cleared his throat, fearing his husky growl might frighten the child. Instead it seemed to quiet her.

The small writhing body stilled. Her blue-green eyes grew wide with fascination. She studied Cub, her gaze seeking and earnest, as if by instinct she knew they shared a bond.

Something seemed to break loose in Cub's being then, something hard and cold that settled to the pit of his stomach. He shuffled forward, the old boots raised like a peace offering. "No, I don't want to take anything from the baby. You keep the boots, Jaycie."

The child glanced back for her mother's approval.

"You don't have to do that, Cub," Alyssa said.

"I want to." A few minutes ago, he hadn't thought he had a single thing to offer Jaycie, except perhaps financial security. Now he wanted to give her the world. It had all changed when he'd looked in her eyes, when she'd looked in his. "If Jaycie wants them, then I want her to have them."

Alyssa set the child down on the floor between them and Cub placed the boots beside the child.

In a flash the red-haired two-year-old plunked her bottom on the ground and poked her fat little legs into the awkwardly oversize boots. She giggled. She sat on the floor and wiggled. She patted the worn, black leather like she might a sleeping pup. Then she tipped her head back, scrunched up her tiny bump of a nose and bestowed on Cub one of the most awesome sights he'd ever seen. She smiled—right at him.

He didn't know what he'd do next. He didn't know how to be a father or what role he'd be allowed to take. He'd mucked things up pretty good already and probably damaged any relationship he might have hoped to have with Alyssa beyond any hope of repair. But he did know one thing, he decided, basking in the glow of his baby daughter's gratitude—no matter what it took, no matter what he had to do, how he had to change or who he had to deal with, he'd do it. He wanted to get to know his child, to get the chance to love her and do everything he could for her, because now that he'd experienced this, he'd walk through fire for another one of those smiles.

"There's more, Cub." Alyssa wanted to place her hand on his arm, to draw his attention away from the baby.

"Huh?" He didn't take his eyes off Jaycie.

"I have more to tell you. We really need to talk."

"Damn right we need to talk," he muttered.

Jaycie shook her legs so that the boot heels thumped on the floor. Then she grinned up at Cub again. "Mine."

"That's right," he whispered. "Mine."

No, *mine!* she wanted to shout. Jaycie was *her* child and up until now she'd never even imagined what it would mean to have to share her, even with Cub. The words petty and selfish immediately sprang to her mind, followed in rapid succession by the justifications, cautious and protective.

How could concern for your child be selfish? she thought. Cub might be Jaycie's father by biology, but in reality he was little more than a stranger to the child.

"The baby likes him." Jaycie stabbed one finger in Cub's direction.

"I think she knows who I am," Cub said in hushed awe.

Alyssa moved close to hover over the child. "Don't be ridiculous. Jaycie likes *anyone* who lets her have her way."

The lie shamed her even as the last harsh tones left her lips. Cub's crushed expression, fleeting as it was, did not make her feel better about her obnoxious overreaction to the very situation she'd prayed for for years.

She knelt beside Jaycie, then looked up at Cub. "I'm

sorry, Cub, that was way out of line. It's just that up until this moment, it's been only the two of us."

She paused to stroke Jaycie's head. The downy red curls seemed to return the gentle caress as they tickled between her fingers and clung to her knuckles. Alyssa dragged in the faint smell of baby powder, leather boots and masculine aftershave and held it for a second. When she exhaled, her secret anxieties rushed out with her breath. "Now, after all this time, you're back in the picture. And I thought I was prepared for that, I thought it would make me happy, for Jaycie's sake. But now that it's a reality, I realize that it creates whole new problems I'd never anticipated, and it makes me feel..."

She didn't know exactly how to explain it, but Cub did.

"It makes you feel like a mama bobcat, protecting her kitten from something unknown," he said.

"Yes," she murmured, amazed by his depth of understanding. "How'd you know that?"

Cub bent at the knees, a grimace flashing over his features for just a split second. With their gazes level, he cocked his head, his hands folded between his open thighs. "I knew that because that's how I feel. I may have just laid eyes on this tiny gal, but I have to tell you, Alyssa, already I'd stand up to anyone or anything to keep her safe. If *anyone* can appreciate your caution about exposing this sweet angel to an old stray hound like me, it's the old stray hound himself."

"Cub?" She reached out to put her hand on the cuff of his shirt. "There's something you should know."

So many things she wanted to say to him, she thought. First, to tell him that she didn't think of him as an "old stray hound" and that she didn't think their daughter needed protection from him, but from the potentially painful situation. And there was that little matter of their marriage still being valid. Mustn't forget that small detail, she admonished herself in a wry moment.

"What is it, Alyssa?"

The wicked sensuality of his hushed, nerve-chafing voice sent a chill down her spine. It didn't ease her heightened response to feel her palm cupped around his wrist, his pulse beating against her fingertips. She tried to focus on her task, her obligation to her child and her child's father, but when her gaze fell into the expectant depths of Cub's eyes, all reason failed.

"I think you should know, Cub—" She tipped her head to one side and, stealing a glance at the happy toddler seated between them, gave a weak smile. "Jaycie is no sweet angel."

"I don't know, Alyssa, she sure looks like a sweet angel to me," Cub whispered twenty minutes later when they'd gotten the baby settled down in her nursery.

Looking down on the pink-cheeked child, fast asleep in her crib, Alyssa felt inclined to agree with Cub. "True, she *looks* all angel, but when she wakes from this nap, get ready for hell on wheels. She's a fistful of dynamite, Cub, just like her—"

She pressed her lips together before she blurted out the obvious conclusion to that. Her fingers gripped the white edge of the baby crib.

Cub cleared his throat.

The room fell so silent she thought she could hear his joints creaking as he shifted his weight.

"Well, we'd better let—"

"Maybe we should—"

They both suddenly spoke at once, neither saying a

thing that mattered or acknowledging the crackling tension in the air.

Three years, at least two secrets and a million hurts lay between them. How could she have expected they could interact as though none of that were so? Alyssa battled down an anxious flutter in her stomach.

She motioned for him to follow her into the hallway, her mind racing on.

All last night, she lay in her bed rehearsing this meeting. Seeing herself as a strong, witty, worldly woman, she would rationally discuss this impossible situation without batting an eye. She'd laugh and shrug and pass it all off as one of life's hard lessons that had left them both weary but stronger for the experience.

*Weary but stronger for the experience.* Those were the exact words she had planned to use. They stood etched in her brain now like a mocking epitaph for her fantasy. What a fool she'd been not to think of how Cub's presence might affect her. She had grown, yes, but no amount of time or "life experience" would change the way she still felt, the way he made her feel when he stood near.

That frightened her. It made her feel vulnerable at a time when she could least afford any weakness. If Cub knew that the annulment had not gone through, what new emotions would that bring, what reactions? In her current shaky state she wondered if she dared risk finding out here and now.

Her daughter's future hung in the balance, she reminded herself, shutting the door to Jaycie's room behind them with a quiet click.

Cub leaned against the gold-flocked wallpaper of the high-ceilinged hall. "Alyssa, I—"

"Cub." She held her hand up to cut him off. "We

have a lot of things to discuss about our circumstances and I have something else important to tell you.''

Cub ran his hand along the sides of his head, his short black hair bristling back into place the instant his fingers whisked over it. ''Darlin', once a man's heard those words, 'You're a father' it's kinda hard for him to absorb much more information.''

She managed a smile at that. ''Thank goodness you feel that way, because I was going to suggest that we continue this discussion later, in a more, um, neutral place.''

''I like that idea.'' His gaze darted around the gaudy hallway, his shoulders lifting to strain against the fresh cotton of his shirt.

''Good.'' She sighed, then folded her hands together. At least he was making this easy, she thought, soothed by a growing gratitude. ''Then why don't I set something up with my lawyer and we can meet in his—''

''Whoa! Lawyer?'' He stepped back as surely as if she pushed him away.

''You agreed to a neutral place, Cub.'' She stood her ground.

''Yeah, but by neutral I meant something like downtown. They're having the rodeo parade tomorrow noon. The craft and food booths open around the square then, too. I figured we could make a day of it, me getting to know my baby girl, you and me talking. You know, relaxed, no pressure, lots of folks around to keep things proper.''

Alyssa's jaw dropped. She took a determined step forward. ''Lots of folks around to keep the rumors circulating, you mean. Do you have any idea the kind of interest you and I together could arouse?''

His cheek tightened on one side. His eyes darkened,

his look smoky with remembered desire. "Indeed I do, darlin'."

Alyssa's knees went as weak as if she'd just dismounted a runaway stallion. She'd never been with any man but the one standing before her. But then, she'd never wanted any man but him. No man could do to her what this one could with a touch, a word, a look.

Her skin went damp and she shivered not from chill but from heat—the heat of her own memories. Even all this time later, she could still envision every detail of Cub's body, every scar and rippling muscle, every movement. Without wanting to, she recalled the way his callused palms rasped against her tender breasts, the way his lips felt exploring her mouth, then her body, just before he—

"No, Cub, no." She blinked, jerked back to her senses by her own embarrassment at letting the memory go too far. She swatted at the air above her warm chest trying not to appear obvious in fanning herself. "We can't go downtown with you. We certainly can't spend the day with you."

"Why not? It's all perfectly innocent." The pink scar along his jaw stretched tight as he flashed a wicked grin.

"No." She shook her head, pleased with the way her new hairdo added a definitive swish to the gesture. "At a parade? Really. That's hardly the kind of place for a serious discussion about the fate of our child, not to mention—"

"Hee-haw, Granddaddy's home!"

Alyssa cringed at the familiar whomp of her father busting in the front door and bellowing up the stairs.

"Whur's my itty-bitty buckaroo?" He howled out the o's of the last word like a crazed coyote.

"Great," Alyssa groaned. "They would have to come home now."

"As show people, the one thing your folks have, darlin', is timing." Cub smiled as if he almost meant it.

"Do I have to remind you that as raised-on-the-ranch show people, the one thing my folks have is a posse mentality and the straight shooting to back it up, *darlin'?*" she whispered. "Do you know how unhappy they're going to be when they find you here again after all this time?"

"Never was afraid of displeasing your folks, Alyssa, and I ain't going to start fretting over it now." He fortified his claim by crossing his bulging arms over his muscular chest. "Living in fear of disappointing Yip and Dolly, that was always your territory."

"*Was* my territory." She laced her arms over her own chest, hugging herself tightly. "A lot has changed now, Cub. My folks don't run my life anymore."

"You just hush yourself up, Yip Cartwright." Despite the sugarcoating of her messages, Dolly packed enough volume in her twanging tone that her words carried up to them. "I swear, you're going to wake that precious punkin up and then Alyssa will have both our hides."

Alyssa gave a satisfied smirk at her mother's seeming confirmation of her newly exerted independence.

"Oh, hooey, that baby would sleep through a cannon volley, if her mama hadn't trained her to need quiet," Yip blustered. "What does a little ol' nervous thing like Alyssa know 'bout babies anyway? I love her more'n I love my next breath but you know, Ma, how that gal'll make a mess of a thing if you don't keep your eye on her."

Alyssa's cheek stung with the heat of her humiliation. Her lower lip trembled. Her throat burned. In three sentences her father had undermined all she'd worked for three years to accomplish, all she had hoped to show Cub she had gained.

"Now, Alyssa," Cub said as softly as his hand felt on her shoulder. "He's only trying to look out for you."

"Look out for me?" The question seethed from her lips like steam hissing from a boiling kettle. "If he was wise, he'd look out for me, all right, because ready or not, here I come."

"Now, granddaddies—they're the ones that know about babies. And I say—"

"Daddy?" Alyssa paused at the top of the stairs, her hand seizing the rail tighter than the reins on an ornery bronc. She aimed her gaze down at the shadowy picture of her parents framed in the redwood-and-leather motif of the foyer.

"Alyssa, honey, that you?" Yip asked, squinting up the stairwell.

"Of course, it's me," she said, punching each syllable in frustrated sarcasm. "I still live here, you know—because I can't afford to move out, not because I can't be trusted to take care of myself and my child."

"Now don't go getting yourself in a tizzy, sugar," Dolly cooed, totally unruffled.

"I'll get myself in a tizzy if I want to, Mother. I'll throw a hissy fit. I'll cuss a blue streak. I'll even have a conniption if that's what it takes to make you two understand that I am not a child anymore." Her voice crescendoed like a ranting maniac's—a completely adult maniac, of course.

"Hee-haw, what got under your saddle, kiddo?" Yip guffawed in his rumbling deep bass.

"I am not a kiddo. I'm a grown woman who makes

her own decisions and takes her lumps, regardless of the mess she makes of things.''

"Shhh. Jaycie's still—''. The sound of Cub's voice only egged her on.

"And I'll thank you, Daddy, not to come into the house hollering like a common ranch rowdy. Don't you know you might wake the baby?''

On cue, a plaintive wail came from Jaycie's nursery.

"See? Are you happy now?'' Alyssa yelled down the stairs.

"The question is, are *you* happy now?'' Cub asked in a tight whisper.

She glanced at him, her husband, the father of her child, the source of the greatest clash in her struggle with her parents for independence, and she smiled. "Not quite yet.''

She turned back to the dim stairwell. "And there's one more thing you two ought to know—Cub Goodacre is back. In fact, he's in this very house right now. And tomorrow, whether you two like it or not, he and I are taking *our* baby to the rodeo parade and spending the whole day in town—*together*.''

## Chapter Five

"Looky there, Jaycie, darlin', your grandma and grandpa are on that float heading down the street." Cub lifted the child high on one shoulder to let her see the last entry, still half a block away, in the Rodeo Days parade.

"Cub, be careful." Alyssa reached up after the baby but did not try to take her away.

"I won't drop her," he muttered. His whole hand fit neatly over Jaycie's middle while his other braced her back, securing her in place.

"Well, you're not exactly an old hand at this. It's not like you know the proper way to handle a child." She defended her concern with a touch of impatience.

"Yeah, well, you've known all your life how to handle a cowboy hat and I don't see you doing a proper job of *that*."

She glanced down at the hat he'd handed her so he could take the baby.

"Oh for..." She released the brim and fit her hand on the crown as she should.

"Good girl." He gave her a nod of approval.

Her eyes narrowed to slits. The fabric of her simple black outfit rustled as she threw back her slender shoulders. She readjusted her grip on the custom-made crown and, for a moment, Cub thought she planned to toss the thing to the ground and perform a Mexican hat dance right on top of it.

Instead, she lifted his hat above her own head and plunked it down, pushing it back so that the low dipping brim didn't block her view. "There. Your treasured hat is safe."

"Well, so's your daughter," he assured her, patting Jaycie's rounded belly.

"Good." Alyssa tipped her chin up; the hat wobbled, then settled low over her eyes, making her look mysterious and seductive.

For one split second, Cub thought about telling her just how appealing he found her wearing his hat that way, with her newfound spunk, sexy haircut and post-baby body.

She pushed the hat to the back of her head and gave him a no-nonsense scowl.

He let that impulse go.

Cub could see that his approval was neither needed nor welcome. And that suited him just fine. Because if she'd answered him with her old sweet smile he might have seen in that a ray of hope. And to a roadsick rodeo warrior like him, even a ray of hope that he might find a life with a woman like Alyssa and with their baby would be enough to sustain his dreams for many years to come. And that was just plain foolhardy.

The baby was the important thing now, caring about

her and being a part of Jaycie's life, not Alyssa's. He'd lost the right to be a part of her life when he refused to compromise about her working and his going back to the rodeo, when she made the arrangements that said he was no longer her husband. He'd never make love to Alyssa again, but for the baby's sake he had to find a way to make peace.

"Hee-haw!" Jaycie shouted and waved her tiny hands at Yip and Dolly as the float came close. The couple beamed thousand-watt smiles and tossed candy from a shimmering replica of a ten-gallon hat, escorted by four fully outfitted prizewinning palominos.

"Heeee-haaaw," Yip brayed back, his face beaming.

"Howdy, Punkin!" Dolly waved right at the child.

Even Cub had to grin at the outrageous pair soaking in the cheers of their kind of folks. Clarence "Yip" Cartwright had always seemed to him a mix of John Wayne at his toughest and some glitter-suited country singer circa 1950-something. Once, while trying to keep up strained small talk with the man, Cub, thinking they'd swap stories about how they came to have their nicknames, had asked why they called him Yip.

"Because, son," Yip answered, pointedly biting out the term to make Cub feel out of line, not one of the family. "That's the sound a fellow makes when he crosses me and I send him packing with his tail between his legs."

Cub hadn't backed down that night and he hadn't backed down last night. He hadn't stayed on in the Cartwrights' home long, but when he left after Alyssa's blowup, he walked out the door, his head high. Yip Cartwright didn't ruffle his feathers, never had, and as for Dolly—

Cub jerked up his chin in a silent salute to the unique woman he'd always admired and cared about.

Dolly Cartwright defied simple description. Weighed down with layers of Native American jewelry that made a distinctive tinkling as she moved, Dolly loved vivid color and subtle manners. Her handcrafted inlaid turquoise watch had no numbers, because Dolly didn't give hoot about the time—she wanted style. And comfort. She wore clothes that stretched to accommodate her ample curves and custom-made boots to fit her wide feet. Add to that black hair streaked with shocking white ratted up enough to add four inches to her height and worn in a long braid down her back and you had Dolly.

Despite their disapproval of his marriage to Alyssa, neither Yip nor Dolly had ever shown him any disrespect personally. Last night, the Cartwrights had been almost deliberately accommodating. While their treatment had surprised him, Cub now believed they realized, as he did, that for Jaycie's sake they all needed to get along.

"Hee-haw!" Jaycie clapped her hands together at the sight of her grandparents passing.

The float moved on, but a pair of the palominos lingered near their spot at the curb of Main Street.

"'Orsies! 'Orsies!" Jaycie squealed, her arms stretched out before her toward the flashy show horses.

Cub chuckled, stealing a glance around the wriggling child to say to Alyssa, "Bet your daddy gave the baby her first pony before she could walk."

"Actually, no." She reached up to ease Jaycie off his shoulder.

"You're kidding." Cub retrieved his hat despite—or was it because of?—the terrific way it looked on his one-time wife.

"'Orsies!'" Jaycie strained in her mother's arms, her entire being focused on the passing animals.

"No, I'm not kidding." Alyssa tried to fit the baby on her hip, but the child squirmed to put herself facing the palominos. "Jaycie does not have a pony. Why would you think she would?"

"Because look at her." He fit his hat down, then bent to put himself level with his daughter. "It's clear she wants one."

Bridles jingling, hooves clopping, the gorgeous animals pranced on by.

"'Orsies! Mine!'"

"You like the horsies, honey?" Cub asked, his heart light at the thought of his next opportunity to delight his child. "Does the baby want a horsie?"

"Cub, no."

"'Orsie!'"

"I won't have it," Alyssa said.

"You don't have to have it," he said, his eyes zeroing in on his child. "It's for Jaycie. How 'bout it, Jaycie? You want Daddy to buy you a pony?"

The small redhead's entire face lit; she grinned that tiny-toothed grin that put a dimple in her cheek and undiluted joy in her daddy's heart.

"Po-ny," she formed the word with relish. "The baby want po-ny."

"Well, if that's what the baby wants, then that's what she's going to have."

"Cotton candy, corn dogs, popcorn, a T-shirt, a personalized marshal's badge, three balloons and a stuffed pony. Cub, you have got to stop buying things for the baby." Alyssa used the last paper napkin they had to wipe the sticky pink goo off Jaycie's fingers.

Cub seized the moment to shift his weight off his hurting hip. They'd walked the vendor-lined streets of Summit City for two hours straight without a break and his body ached from every agonizing footfall. Luckily, Alyssa had let him push Jaycie's stroller, which gave him something to lean on. Otherwise, he'd have never made it this far.

Of course, seeing people make the obvious connection between him and the baby had eased his discomfort considerably. He'd never felt this kind of overwhelming pride, not even when he won a championship. The pure pleasure he found in watching the baby discover new things led him to a discovery of his own. He wasn't the same man who had let pride and fear of ruining another woman's life keep him from working things out with Alyssa. Two years ago, he doubted if would have been ready for this, but now, seasoned by success bought with loneliness and heartache, Cub now felt that maybe he had it in him to be a decent father.

And he had the money to do right by Jaycie, as well. He'd taken as much delight today in spoiling her as the baby had taken in being spoiled. Yes, he admitted to himself that he was spoiling her but then, he had a right to, didn't he? Later, when he and Alyssa had worked out the details of how they would share their responsibilities for the child, then he'd buckle down and be the strict father.

Yeah, right. He'd known his daughter for twenty-four hours and she already had him wrapped securely around her little finger.

Alyssa straightened away from cleanup duty and tossed the napkin in a nearby trash can.

Cub wondered if Alyssa had noticed the change in him. Not that he hoped she'd see him as husband material again; much as his heart longed for a second chance there, he hardly deserved it. But he did hope she could see in him the potential to play an important role in Jaycie's life.

He smiled at the now groggy toddler clutching the stuffed pony like a pillow to her cheek. The image made his heart swell.

And the image of her mother, licking her fingertips one by one to clean away the sweet-smelling, sticky remnants of cotton candy, that image inspired other things.

Alyssa inspected the last bits of pink clinging to her knuckle, then placed it between her full lips.

Cub watched like a starving man witnessing the last scrap of food disappear at a banquet he'd just missed.

She finished, dabbed at the corner of her mouth, then looked at him. "Cub? Is something wrong?"

*Just about every danged thing in the world,* he wanted to say. He shook his head.

"Hey, Cub! Cub Goodacre, you sorry ol' son of a—"

"Price Wellman!" Cub slapped his palm into his old friend's offered hand and gave it a firm shake. "Haven't seen you since I had that bad wreck, few years back."

"Yep." Price, a tall man who sported a five-o'clock shadow at two in the afternoon, ducked his head and scratched his jaw. "Sorry about backing out on our big plans to get up a ranching outfit like that, Cub. We just couldn't spare the money then."

Cub rolled off a lazy shrug. "Couldn't be helped."

"And it did all seem to work out for the best," Price added. "If you'd settled down back then rodeo would have lost one hell of a bull-rider. Been following your exploits with Diablo's Heartbreak and—is that Alyssa I see?"

A twinge of pain shot through Cub's tight neck muscles as he glanced back at Alyssa pushing the stroller up to them.

"Hi, Price. How are you doing?" She nodded.

"I'm fine, but I don't seem to be doing half as good as this cowboy." He jerked his head toward Cub.

The reference to his precarious career made Cub self-conscious, so he changed the subject. "So, Price, I heard you and your family moved about twenty miles south of your folks' place?"

"Yep, soon as I got back on my feet, we bought a little piece of land and a house. The wife turned it into a bed-and-breakfast."

"Now that's sweet." Cub chuckled. "Living off your wife's business."

"Very funny." Price punched Cub in the arm. "I tend to upkeep of the place and we board horses. I run some trail rides, help sponsor the Junior Rodeo every year. The wife sees to the guests."

"So, it's a real partnership," Alyssa surmised, nailing Cub with a sidelong glance.

"Yes, ma'am." Price nodded.

Cub braced himself, stiff-armed, on the sturdy handle of the baby stroller, trying to pretend he wasn't working on deciphering the unspoken meaning of Alyssa's remark.

"But it looks like you two know a thing or two about teamwork." He peered down at Jaycie, who had dozed off.

Alyssa pressed her lips together, her cheeks flaming at Price's implication.

"Yeah, well." Cub caught her around the shoulder and drew her to him to keep her from embarrassing all three of them with a hostile denial. "You know how it is."

"Sure." Price nodded.

Alyssa tensed beneath his arm but she kept her peace and for that he was thankful. For the way her nearness made him feel, he was less appreciative. He forced from his mind the way her soft body pressed to his, the temptation to pull her closer until he could feel the warmth of her breasts through the thin cotton of his shirt and said, "Good running into you after all this time, Price."

"Sure is, buddy." He snorted a quick laugh. "Who'd have thought it three years ago that instead of heading up our own outfit by now, I'd be standing in line to buy candy apples for my kids and you'd be pushing a baby carriage?"

Cub faked a laugh. In reality he didn't think one damn bit of this was funny.

"So, does this mean you're finally settling down?" Price pointed to the stroller. "Hope it isn't because the rumors I've heard are true."

"What rumors?" Alarm colored Alyssa's tone.

"No rumors. You know how much trash talk makes the rounds of the rodeo circuit." Cub flexed his fingers into her upper arm, giving Price a glare that would have made a coyote back down.

He knew he would have to tell Alyssa about his medical condition, but not now. When he'd made his last ride, gone out on top of his game, then he could face her with it and not risk suffering her pity. They had enough to deal with now, anyway, without involving her in something no one could change. It was his injury and he alone would deal with it.

He slipped his arm from Alyssa's shoulder and gave Price a farewell handshake. "You take care of yourself, Price."

"And say hello to your family for me," Alyssa added, as Cub turned to push the stroller in the other direction.

"Will do, Alyssa. We'll be rooting for your ride this weekend, Cub," Price called after them.

"Well, you seemed in a hurry to scoot away from him." Alyssa caught up and matched his stride.

"Said all I had to say. Why stand around jawing?"

She clucked her tongue at him.

Good. He'd rather she was disgusted by his lack of manners than too curious about those rumors. He leaned more heavily on the stroller until it squawked quietly beneath his weight. "Why don't we find a shady spot to sit a while and talk?"

Alyssa glanced around them. "I'd feel better if we kept walking."

"'Course you would." His eyes sought out an empty park bench.

"What was that?"

"I see a great spot over there." He started to push the stroller forward but Alyssa stepped into his path.

"Listen here, Cub, I am not going to sit down now."

"But, Alyssa—"

"No. It's not open to debate." She held her hand up. "This is just isn't the right time or place for me to say the things I need to say to you."

"But, Alyssa—"

"Whether you like it or not the new, independent Alyssa has no intention of whistling to your tune ever again." She shook her hair back.

"But—"

"There are no buts, Cub, I'll sit down and talk when the time is right for me, not when you decree it so. You got that?"

"Hey, hey, truce." He cocked his head and pushed

his hat back so that she could see the sincerity clearly in his eyes. "I'm not trying to force anything, darlin'. I just wanted to take a break, maybe catch up on a few things, sit and look at our baby a while."

"Oh." Her breasts rose and fell in one tightly controlled sigh. The rosy color of her cheeks hinted at whatever chagrin she might feel. Her gaze dipped. "Guess I jumped to the wrong conclusion, Cub."

"It happens."

He hadn't meant it as an indictment, but the sadness of her smile, the regret in her tone made it clear she took it that way. "Maybe I have misjudged you this time. It's just that our past experience and your cockamamie idea about buying Jaycie a pony when I absolutely forbid her to have one—"

"Oh, Jaycie's pony. That reminds me." He cupped his hand to the side of his mouth in hopes his voice would carry over the crowd noise. "Hey, Price?"

Price pivoted on his boot heel from the line outside the candy apple cart. "What can I do for you, buddy?"

"You know anyone in these parts, has a real gentle pony—" he slashed his hand through the air to indicate the approximate size "—for sale?"

"Then again, maybe I didn't misjudge you at all," Alyssa seethed at his back. "Maybe you're still every ounce the domineering jackass you always were."

"Now what did I do?" he muttered as watched her struggle to push the stroller through the enveloping crowd, away from him.

She had to be out of her mind. That was the only viable explanation, Alyssa decided. For a few minutes there—she shut her eyes and made herself confront the truth—*all day long,* she had secretly been thinking, hoping, believing that she, Jaycie and Cub could become a family again.

*What an idiot she was!* She clenched her teeth, thinking back on the chain of events that had led to this moment.

All she had wanted, all she still wanted, was to find a quiet, safe place to have a mature discussion with Cub about their situation. But had that happened? No. Instead they were spending the day as Cub had suggested.

Sure, she accepted her role in the way things turned out, but deep down she knew that Cub had manipulated circumstances so that they'd do things his way, not hers, not theirs but *his*. Cub hadn't changed—mellowed maybe, but deep down beneath that quiet, humble surface beat the heart of the same benevolent tyrant.

"Does the baby want a pony?" she mimicked. "Well, if that's what the baby wants then that's what the baby is going to have—over my dead body."

"Hee-haw!"

Alyssa froze; she turned her gaze skyward. "There's the cocktail onion on the hot-fudge-and-bacon-lard sundae this day has become—my folks."

"Alyssa, baby, there you are!" Alyssa's mother waved, her bracelets clanking as they collided in a downward slide along her raised arm.

She thought for a moment about running, but knowing Cub would be closing in from behind and with her parents standing at the end of the street like gunslingers at high noon, she had no idea where to go.

"Hi, Mama." She gave a limp wave back.

"What happened to that man o' yours? He up and disappear again?" Leave it to her daddy to shout out something so personal in a crowded street of their tiny town.

Most kids, she had read in a parenting book, outgrew feeling embarrassed in public by their folks after adolescence. It was, for the most part, a short developmental phase. Alyssa stared at the bedazzled pair cutting a swath through the crowd. Yip ham-handed total strangers with arm-wrenching handshakes. Dolly, smiling like the Queen of England, looked—and jingled—like a box full of broken Christmas ornaments. Alyssa wondered if her "short developmental phase" might be one for the record books.

She clenched her teeth, determined not to play into her mortification and frustration by shouting back a denial of her connection to Cub that no one, not even she, would believe. Besides, she could just imagine herself shouting out some shrewish thing about Cub just as the man strolled up to her side. *That* was the kind of luck she'd had all week.

She glanced behind her to check Cub's progress through the crowd, then swiveled her head around to see how her parents were faring as they "pressed the flesh" on their way to her. For one surrealistic moment, she could empathize with those movie characters that found themselves trapped in some airless dungeon with spiked walls slowly moving in on them. At the last minute, those fictional characters detected a way out, a means of escape. That's where the similarities ended, because Alyssa had no way out but through.

She'd have to get through a second meeting between her parents—with their fear that Cub might take their precious grandbaby—and the man who didn't even realize that their valid marriage gave him that option. Guilt pangs, pangs that grew more intense with each passing hour that she held her secret, made her chest constrict and her temples throb. She gritted her teeth, wondering how she would survive without making another mistake—in front of the three people who seemed, to her, constantly on alert for her next big screwup.

"Alyssa, wait up, I don't know what I said back there that set you off, but—" Cub's uneven gait brought him within a foot of her before he pulled up short. "Didn't realize you'd met up with your folks. Hello, Dolly, Yip."

"How-do, Jacob." Yip jerked his head upward instead of giving a respectful cowboy nod. "I was just asking Alyssa here if you'd run off and—"

"Never mind that, *Clarence.*" Dolly poked an elbow in her husband's side, her jewelry making it sound as if she'd shattered a glass rib. Still, the brittle tension remained intact between the two men.

"Was talking to a man about a horse, if you must know, Yip." Cub placed his hand on the stroller.

"This isn't the time or place for a family powwow." Independent, take-charge Alyssa to the rescue. "Let's say we—"

"A horse?" Yip scoffed. "Thought you just dealt in bull, Goodacre."

Cub exhaled a short huff of air from his nostrils. His scarred jaw ticked. "The horse ain't for me, not that it's any of your lookout, Cartwright. It's for the baby."

"Now hold it right there." Alyssa held up her hand. "Cub, I thought I made it very clear that I don't want Jaycie to have a pony."

"For the baby?" Her father's expression softened toward Cub for the first time since—well, ever. "Well, why didn't you say so, man? Been trying to get this tyke on a pony for a solid year now, maybe more."

"You have?" Cub spoke to her father as though she'd suddenly turned invisible—and inaudible.

"Yes, he has and there's a reason why he hasn't succeeded. I won't let him." Alyssa drew her shoulders up to make her presence better felt. "Jaycie is my child and I say—"

"Well, I just had a word with Price Wellman. They've got a couple tame Shetlands and they might want to turn loose of one. Ought to be a good safe mount for Jaycie to start out on."

"I don't care if he's got gigantic trained turtles equipped with air bags and seat belts. Jaycie is *my* daughter and I say—"

"That Price is a good man," Dolly said.

"Knows his horseflesh," Yip added, his ruddy cheeks rounded with a grin. "If he says a pony would do for the baby, then that's good enough for me."

"Well, it's not good enough for me." Alyssa angled her shoulder between her parents and Cub, her breath coming in shallow, angry puffs. She'd be darned if this trio was going to exclude her so easily. "I have my reasons for not wanting horses and ranch stuff pushed on my child. I want her to have the chance to make up her own mind about what she wants, when she's old enough to know—"

"What kind of money is he wanting?" Yip folded his arms over his barrel chest as if Alyssa hadn't said a thing.

"Fair market," Cub replied. "But money isn't a worry, Yip. Long as I'm around, Jaycie won't want for anything, I'll see to that."

"*I* already see to that." Alyssa's voice cracked under the strain building in her body from having her wishes so blatantly ignored.

"Glad to hear that, Cub," Yip said the nickname with a warmth she'd never him heard use toward Cub before.

"Not that we mind putting in for her care," Dolly said, hugging her husband's arm. "We'd do just about anything for that child."

"Crawl buck naked through a cactus patch," Yip blustered as evidence to the pains he'd suffer for his grandbaby. "Fight a grizzly with nothing but a popgun and butter knife."

"Wear plastic clip-on earrings," Dolly added dreamily, only straightening up and explaining when the men gave her a strange look. "You know, so Jaycie can tug them off and teethe on them."

"Ah." Both men spoke and nodded in unison.

"Excuse me, but I am the one who takes care of Jaycie." Alyssa tapped her finger to her chest.

From the looks her parents and Cub gave her, she supposed she might just as well stand on one foot and sing "I'm a little teapot" than try to defend herself. Still, she went on, her voice gaining momentum like a boulder thundering down a mountainside. "I work, you know. I've held a job since she was six months old and in case you've forgotten, I am a full partner in Crowder and Cartwright. And I have the bank loan to prove it."

"Bank loan?" That got Cub's attention.

"Yes, that's how most businesses start up, with capital from a loan they repay as the profits grow." Alyssa started to twist her finger in her hair but caught the habit at the last minute and gripped the stroller handle instead.

"I got news for you, darlin'." Cub clutched the stroller handle tighter, his fingers flexing next to hers as if jockeying for control. "Bankers expect you to repay that loan whether or not you show any profits at all."

"I told her…" Yip let his words trail off to imply the insinuated doom awaiting Alyssa's foolishness.

Dolly rolled her eyes and even that simple gesture,

the slightest jiggle of her head, made her necklaces give off a quiet metallic whisper.

Cub's movement agitated her. The tone of her father's voice and the sound of her mother's jewelry rasped against Alyssa's frayed nerves.

"Wish you'd come back before she signed them gawd-awful papers, son." Yip shook his head.

"What difference would that have made?" Alyssa demanded, her breathing heavy but steady, still controlling her anger and humiliation over being treated like a five-year-old.

"World of difference," Yip said. "Since he coulda put a stop to it flat out."

"Well, now I don't see how, Yip. Alyssa is a grown woman with ideas of her own, and even if I don't approve of them or would have her do things another way, that just doesn't have anything to do with me anymore."

Even though Cub clearly wasn't jumping on the bandwagon to belittle her, Alyssa could not so easily turn off her sweeping irritation at him as well as her folks. His admitting that he didn't approve, that he "would have her do things another way" was just a sugarcoated way of saying that, given the chance, he'd run roughshod over her wishes and dreams again. All in her best interest, of course, she thought bitterly.

"You don't see how you could have stopped her?" Yip barked a belly laugh. "Now that's a knee-slapper, son. You could have brought the barn down around her ears if you'd gotten here in time."

"That's enough, Daddy. Don't go mixing in with my business, I warn you." The tremble in Alyssa's legs was pure adrenaline, not fear. She stood ready to challenge her insecurities, her husband's penchant for control and her daddy at the same time.

"Alyssa has a point, sir." Cub's voice rumbled soft and deep. He shifted his feet so that his body swayed like a subtle cowboy swagger.

"Oh, no, you don't." Alyssa shot him a look warning him to back down. "Don't you go stepping in trying to fight my battles for me, Cub. You don't have that right."

"'Course he does," Yip blustered. "That's as it should be."

"Daddy, don't say another—"

"I don't have any rights in regards to Alyssa anymore, Yip." Cub eased his grip on the stroller handle and stood firm beside her.

"Balderdash!" If Yip were a tobacco-chewing man, he'd have spit just then for emphasis.

"Clarence, really—"

"Daddy, don't." Her heart thrashed in her chest, heat scalded her neck and cheeks. She knew what was coming next. Like a terrible storm rolling in from the hills, she could see the disaster looming and yet could do nothing to stop it.

"You got every right in the world, Jacob. Every right due a man legally married, but—"

A deathly stillness swathed her ears as her total frustration over the events of the entire day swelled to the boiling point in her head. Her flight toward independence now spiraled out of control, heading for a fiery crash, she supposed, when Cub would stake his claim to Jaycie and she could lose everything that mattered to her.

She turned toward Cub, more enraged than frightened, her every maternal instinct on point, ready to lash out.

"Married?" Cub whispered the question with such intense quiet that she doubted if anyone else even heard it.

When Alyssa replied, though, it was loud enough for her intrusive parents, her domineering husband and half the town to hear. "Yes, but don't get any ideas about what rights that gives you to Jaycie. We may still be married now but we won't be for long because, Cub Goodacre, I want a divorce."

# Chapter Six

"This is how I find out I'm still a married man? When you demand a divorce by shouting it to me in the middle of a street carnival?" Each syllable spoken scraped the raw edges of Cub's battered emotions.

"Cub, not here." Alyssa met his gaze with her head high and her arms crossed.

"Oh, I see." He shut out the waves of murmuring rolling over the bystanders within earshot of their exchange. "This is the right place for you to demand a divorce but it's the wrong place for me to ask you what the hell you're talking about?"

"Listen here, you two—" Yip stepped forward.

Alyssa threw one hand up to stop her father. "I think we've listened to you enough for the moment, Daddy. This is my problem and I will handle it. But if you really want to be of some help, then please take Mama and Jaycie and go home."

"That's a fine idea, Clarence." Dolly strode up to

take command of the stroller and, by her attitude, her husband as well.

The curious crowd parted to allow the grandparents and sleeping child to wheel away from the mess they'd helped create. Still, the prying eyes remained on Alyssa and Cub. Anticipation of their next move electrified the air in the swarming street. It felt as real as the pungent mingling smells of cotton candy, hot dogs roasting and the axle grease from the nearby rides.

Cub snagged Alyssa by the arm, then began to push his way toward the sidewalk.

"What do you think you're doing?" she demanded, her flat shoes dragging on the street as she resisted his prompting.

"I'm moving us to a better place to have this discussion."

"What if I don't want to move?"

He stopped and bent his neck so that their eyes met in a smoldering glare. "It was your idea, darlin'. You said, and I quote, 'Not here.' If we ain't having this talk here, then that means we have to move, because we *are* having this talk, Alyssa. It's already long overdue."

To her credit, she didn't whine or pout but pulled her shoulders up and came along.

The bystanders whispered, some chuckled, a few pointed, but none stood in their way as he escorted his wife inside his hotel. His *wife*. The thought made his heart beat as if it was trying to push his pulse through a knot.

"The elevator is this way," he muttered, wishing his hat afforded him the sanctuary the low-dipped brim suggested. "Let's just hope we can get through the lobby without anyone noticing me."

"The stairs would be more secluded," Alyssa started toward the door marked Stairway.

Cub held his ground, causing her to jerk back and stumble into his side.

Pain ripped through his body from his leg to his ribs. He sucked in his breath and helped her right herself. The hot stabbing sensation lingered after he'd eased her weight off his body. Still, he preferred that to the excruciating effort it would take to get up those stairs.

He had enough to deal with just now without getting into the history and prognosis for his half-shot hip. He was in no mood for that distraction or the pityfest from Alyssa that would follow. Under the circumstances, the last thing on earth he wanted right now was for Alyssa to learn about his career-threatening injury.

"We'll take the elevator." He lurched toward the twin sets of gleaming silver doors.

"Whatever *you* say." It rang with pure accusation.

Cub jabbed his finger into the "up" button.

Both of them stared at the lit numbers above the doors, but the numbers did not change.

Alyssa leaned forward and punched the button again and again. The doors swished open. She marched in ahead of him as if she alone had called the elevator to them.

Neither of them said a word on the ride up the elevator. Or when he cranked the key in the door, then pushed it open. Or when they both stepped inside the impersonal box of a room, a fancy box, but a box all the same.

The heavy door fell shut with a regulated whoosh and a click of the automatic lock.

One of them had to be the first to speak. Since she'd been the one keeping the secret, Cub thought it should rightfully be Alyssa. And so he stood, just inside the door, watching her.

She touched the TV remote, then the big ashtray holding some change and the yellow flyer he hadn't unfolded since finding it on her porch. She lifted her head to take a quick peek out of the tall window with the afternoon light streaming in; she pretended the western artwork, in its muted golds and browns caught her eye. She walked the length of the room, pivoted, stopped in her tracks at the foot of the oversize bed, then finally spoke.

"Cub?"

He braced himself for her explanation, not sure he could bear hearing it. "What is it, Alyssa?"

"Why is there a cane propped up beside your bed?"

*Gotcha.* Cub could just imagine some cosmic comedian laughing his butt off over this little incident. He'd nearly walked himself crippled trying to keep Alyssa from knowing about his injury, then led her right to the place where she'd see his cane. Luckily, his other medical supplies were tossed in the closet.

"The cane is a precaution. I got a little…bruised on my last ride. No big deal. Not like I use it, you'll notice."

She scrunched her nose up. "I never saw a cowboy use a cane for a bruise before."

"Yeah, well, you probably never saw a cowboy with a sports-medicine specialist on his payroll, either. But that's the way we rodeo these days."

She pursed her lips. She just wasn't buying it, he thought. Rather than give her time to question him, he went on the offensive.

"But we didn't come here to discuss my health, Alyssa. We came here to talk about the annulment." His rough voice made Alyssa go stock-still.

Her whole attitude changed before his eyes, softened, yet grew stronger.

"There never was an annulment." She couldn't look at him, even though her tone showed no shame at what she had done. "You'd have known that if you had, even once, opened a letter I'd sent. If you had bothered to call me, just to see how things stood."

That was why she didn't feel ashamed, Cub realized; she had no reason to. He alone shouldered the blame for this kick-in-the-gut response tearing up his insides.

He took a staggering step toward the bed. He needed to sit. He needed to sort his physical agony from his emotional one by lessening the one he could control. Even as he lowered himself to the firm mattress, the pressure on his hip relented and he sighed in relief.

She turned her face profile to him. "Why, Cub? Why didn't you read the letters I sent?"

His lips twitched. He dragged the back of his hand along jaw and neck. The familiar ridge of scar tissue stretched taut as he scowled over her question.

"The truth." She turned to face him. "This is the time for bare-bones truth, and you know it. I can take it, Cub, I don't need you to protect me from it."

He snorted. "Yeah, but how do I protect myself?"

"What?" She brushed her hair from her shoulder, her fingers trembling as they tangled in the soft layers for just a second before she dropped her hand. "What are you talking about, Cub?"

"The truth, that's what you wanted, isn't it?" He pushed the words out through clenched teeth. "And the truth is, I didn't open your letters because I was afraid."

"Afraid? You?" Her laughter was genuine.

He shifted his eyes. Slowly, he gripped the crown of

his hat, lifted it from his head and laid it down on the table beside the bed.

She cleared her throat and folded her arms over her black shirt. "What in the world would you be afraid of? Getting the annulment papers?"

"No, I figured that was a done deal." He leaned forward, his hands clasped between his knees.

"Afraid of what, then?"

*Afraid.* Each time she threw his own word back at him, driving home just another of his many shortcomings, he flinched. Weariness and pain melded with the shock and anxiety within him. All that was reflected in his clipped, unforgiving tone when he asked, "Alyssa, do you recall that last time we spoke on the phone?"

She blinked.

He could see her shudder at the waves of harsh memory assaulting her.

"You mean the argument?" she whispered.

"That was no argument," he said, tugging his lips up into a half smile. "That was a wake-up call."

"I...I don't understand." Her strawberry-blond hair rustled over her tight shoulders.

The bed creaked as he settled in, stretching one leg out. "What is it your daddy always says about your picking a man?"

Her forehead puckered at the strange question, but she answered. "Love any boy but a cowboy?"

He nodded to encourage her.

"Marry any man but a rodeo man," she finished in a faraway, little-girl voice.

"And that goes double for Cub Goodacre," Cub concluded.

"Daddy never said that."

"You knew he would have said it if he'd ever suspected we were thinking of running off to get married. You see, your daddy knew."

"Knew what?"

He bowed his head. Was he a coward not to face her when he said it? The battle raging in his veins, in his mind, in his being, told him no. Some enemies are better faced by lowering your head and charging on, the way a bull goes after the source of his torment. "Your daddy knew, and I knew, in my heart, if I'd only admitted it. I knew all along, Alyssa, and our...argument only showed me that you'd finally figured it out, too. A man like me...me in particular, I'm no good for a woman like you."

"Cub, that's just not true." The force of her denial propelled her toward him. She took two unsteady steps before he held his hand up.

"Don't. Denying it will only make things worse in the long run, especially now that I know that we're still—" He raised his face. "Legal."

"Married," she murmured.

"Yes, married."

She laid her left hand over his right and without realizing it until he'd done it, Cub glanced at the finger once circled by his ring. The finger was bare.

He tore his gaze away.

"Is that why you didn't open the letters, Cub? You feared they'd be full of the same awful venom as that argument?"

"I carry every word of that last conversation with me to this day, like the broken tip of a knife lodged in my chest. You think I wanted letters, too? Letters that I would carry all the days of my life to remind me of how I failed you, of all the ways I let you down?"

"Didn't you ever think those letters might carry an

# GET A FREE TEDDY BEAR...

You'll love this plush, cuddly Teddy Bear, an adorable accessory for your dressing table, bookcase or desk. Measuring 5 ½" tall, he's soft and brown and has a bright red ribbon around his neck – he's completely captivating! And he's yours *absolutely free*, when you accept this no-risk offer!

# AND TWO FREE BOOKS!

Here's a chance to get **two free Silhouette Romance® novels** from the Silhouette Reader Service™ **absolutely free!**

There's no catch. You're under no obligation to buy anything. We charge nothing – ZERO – for your first shipment. And you don't have to make any minimum number of purchases – not even one!

Find out for yourself why thousands of readers enjoy receiving books by mail from the Silhouette Reader Service. They like the **convenience of home delivery**…they like getting the best new novels months before they're available in bookstores…and they love our **discount prices!**

Try us and see! Return this card promptly. We'll send your free books and a free Teddy Bear, under the terms explained on the back. We hope you'll want to remain with the reader service – but the choice is always yours! (U-SIL-R 04/98)      **215 SDL CF4Q**

NAME

ADDRESS                                                    APT.

CITY                              STATE              ZIP

Offer not valid to current Silhouette Romance® subscribers. All orders subject to approval.

©1993 HARLEQUIN ENTERPRISES LIMITED                        **Printed in U.S.A.**

▶ CLAIM YOUR FREE BOOKS AND FREE GIFT! RETURN THIS CARD TODAY! ▶

# NO OBLIGATION TO BUY!

If offer card is missing write to: Silhouette Reader Service, 3010 Walden Ave., P.O. Box 1867, Buffalo, NY 14240-1867

**BUSINESS REPLY MAIL**
FIRST-CLASS MAIL    PERMIT NO. 717    BUFFALO, NY

POSTAGE WILL BE PAID BY ADDRESSEE

SILHOUETTE READER SERVICE
3010 WALDEN AVE
PO BOX 1867
BUFFALO NY 14240-9952

NO POSTAGE
NECESSARY
IF MAILED
IN THE
UNITED STATES

apology for my hateful words? A chance for reconciliation?''

"You mean a chance to postpone the inevitable?"

She shook her head.

"Don't you see, Alyssa? I sent those letters back because one way or another they could only bring more pain and sorrow, more loss."

"You're wrong, Cub." She moved to the edge of the bed. "If you had read those letters, things might be better for both of us right now. They certainly would be for Jaycie."

"Jaycie." He rubbed his hands over his face, coughing out a hard laugh. "Just what I deserved, huh? Another female that needs my help and protection. What are the odds of me pulling that off without another disaster?"

"Pretty damned good—if you get one thing straight."

Okay, she had his attention, she realized. Now if she could just reach past that cowboy mentality and make a connection. She stepped closer until her black jeans snagged the deep gold of the bedspread. Glancing down, she made a hasty decision and lowered herself to sit on the corner of the bed.

Her impulsive move did not alter Cub's expression, but his breathing grew more pronounced, coming heavy, in a quickened pace. His eyes reflected a pain so real she imagined it was almost physical.

That passed, replaced in an instant with a look more familiar to her. A dark wanting from deep within the only man she knew well enough to appreciate his longing.

Even now she remembered the feeling of his body, his muscles so taut her fingers could not sink into his flesh but only curl into a ball against his back, his arms.

She remembered the tickling of his coarse black hair against her palms, the smell of his skin when his neck pressed against her lips during lovemaking. She remembered—everything.

She braced her arm straight against the hard mattress.

He lowered his chin, his eyes hooded, his scarred jaw clenched.

If she slid her hand, so that her body stretched out across the bed beside him, he would do the rest. She saw as much in his hungry look. Her breath filled her upper chest with damp thickness.

He swallowed. His boot heel scraped the carpeted floor as he extended one leg. His gaze bored into hers as if he was waiting for her to make the first move.

The idea tempted her, the way a fire fascinates despite its potential for destruction. If she had only herself to consider, Alyssa thought, touching her cool fingertips to her warm neck, she'd do it. Just like that. She'd lay herself down and take what Cub offered, however fleeting and heartbreaking it might prove.

But she had to think of the baby. That snapped her out of her compelling but wistful haze. For Jaycie's sake she could never allow herself to act on those wayward desires. Even a kiss would give too much, because it would give credence to Cub's already archaic concept of relationships.

She could do nothing that might lead him to think he could come in and start running her life—and in turn, Jaycie's. She must do everything within her power to do just the opposite, to show him she would make her own way and that was the example she wanted set for their daughter.

"This is the way I see it, Cub." Alyssa cleared her

throat, her no-nonsense tone locking them back in reality.

He exhaled hard, then gave a curt nod.

"Jaycie *does* need your help and protection," she said. "That's because she is a child, not because she's female and you are the big he-man provider."

She puffed herself up and pounded her chest.

Despite it all, Cub let go of a laugh, then a cleansing sigh. "Still, I wish I had been here for Jaycie from the git-go, Alyssa. There's no denying I was a poor excuse for a son, as a lover and a husband, I don't want to fail as a father."

"You won't, Cub." She smiled. "And while I know your relationship with your mom wasn't…nurturing, you were the child. You were still a child when you left home, for that matter. It wasn't your job to watch out for your mother—it should have been the other way around."

"I can tell myself that but that but it doesn't help my mom much, does it?"

She dropped that line of reasoning, knowing she could not make any headway there and decided to talk about the things she could address with authority. "You aren't a failure as a husband, either. Whatever failures this marriage has had, they've been pretty mutual."

He didn't roll his eyes at that, but she could tell he wanted to. His lips stayed in a tight line but she could hear his message in his expression. He thought her naive, innocent, still the shy, inexperienced girl he'd married.

That reaction galled her. She pulled her body straight, prepared to show him that he was dealing with a mature woman now. "And as for being a failure as a lover—"

He arched an eyebrow.

She lowered her lashes and smiled. "I don't recall registering any complaints in that department."

He gave an amused huff.

Not exactly the reaction she'd wanted.

He shook his head and groaned out a resigned sigh. "Actually, darlin', I was referring to my first lover."

"You mean what's-her-name?" She tossed her head and leaned back on one elbow, hoping he read that as a sophisticated nonchalance about his past.

"Yeah," he chuckled, obviously still not wowed by her act. "I didn't exactly do ol' what's-her-name any favors."

"I'm sure she enjoyed the ride." She reached out to put her hand on his, thinking, how's *that* for a worldly-wise response? "Besides, from my point of view she did a hell of a lot more of a number on you than you did on her."

His humor faded.

"I don't feel so sorry for her, and neither should you, Cub."

"Why not?" His eyes narrowed.

"Didn't you know?" She gave a throaty laugh she didn't really feel. "She wrote a raunchy tell-all book about sex on the rodeo circuit and made a bundle."

"Oh?"

"I hear she got a whole chapter out of you." She pursed her lips hoping to look pouting and sexy rather than jealous and insecure over it. "So, maybe you didn't let her down as much as you thought."

"Guess she got some kind of support from me after all, then," he said.

Was that a personal revelation or a jab at her, implying that a woman needed a man—one way or another?

"I guess she did, indirectly." She sat up and crossed

her arms. "But don't forget she did all the work, um, writing the book, that is."

"And doing the research," he added, not so helpfully.

"Nevertheless, she did the work and it's to her credit." Alyssa stood, glaring down at Cub. "She did not depend on a man to shelter and support her."

"Okay, okay." He held his hands up.

"My point about both those examples is that people are ultimately responsible for themselves." She tucked a strand of hair behind her ear. "You can't save someone from themselves if they don't want your help."

"I can agree with that." He fit his hand over his knee, using that support to lean toward her and say softly, "But I also know that it isn't so awful to accept help when you need it."

She whisked the side of her hand to flick invisible lint from her black sleeve. "If that's directed at me, then I have to tell you the only thing I need your help on right now is getting a divorce—"

"Whoa, gal!"

"Don't you tell me to whoa, Cub." She tried to remember the way she'd written it in her letter to him. "I've waited a long time for you to come back so I could find some closure for this part of my life. I don't want to postpone it any longer. I'm ready for my new life to begin."

"Geez, Alyssa, cut me some slack on this, will ya?" He pushed at the bed as if to get up, then hesitated, and stayed put. "Three days ago I blew into town focused on dealing with one thing, having to make one of the best rides of my career tomorrow night."

She'd forgotten about his ride, that some mean-tempered bull had brought him back to town, not love for her or even the letter she'd written to him and cast to the wind.

"In this short time I've learned I have a daughter, I'm still married and you want a divorce. I just can't focus on it all at one time."

"You're right." She hung her head. Her stomach knotted with regret at pushing it all so hard, so fast. "You deserve time to think about all this, to let it settle in. Maybe it would be best for both of us if we didn't see each other until after the rodeo."

"Well, I didn't mean for it to go that far. That is, I'd like to spend time with…" He shifted his weight in clear discomfort.

Alyssa felt a surge of pride at jumping in to rescue him for a change. "Of course, you can see Jaycie as much as you'd like while you're in town. Just call the ranch and I'll arrange for you two to spend time alone whenever you like."

"Fine." He folded and unfolded his hands, then gazed toward the window.

She thrummed her fingers against her leg. "Well, I guess if that's settled, then—"

"About the pony—"

"No. No pony, Cub." She broadened her stance as if readying for battle. "I won't have Jaycie pushed the way I was. When she's old enough, she can chose her own course. I won't allow you or my father to try to force her into a mold that may or may not fit her."

Whether he understood her position or not, Cub agreed to it with a nod.

"Well, I'd like to do something for her."

"She doesn't need a thing, Cub."

"She needs a father."

No response seemed adequate to that, so she gave none.

"And I need to be a father, Alyssa. I haven't been there for her up to now and I'm not real sure how good I'll be at it now that I am here, but I do know this—I can provide for her and well. I make a damn fine living and I'll gladly give you whatever—"

"I can't take your money, Cub." She stepped back, her hands up. "I won't."

"Not even for Jaycie's sake?"

"It's for Jaycie's sake I won't take it. I'm her role model, Cub. I want to set an example for her of a strong independent woman who earns her keep and doesn't look to a daddy or a husband to take care of her."

"I wouldn't be much of a father if I didn't take care of my little girl financially."

"I'll accept a reasonable child support, Cub. Nothing more." She took another step back. "And nothing for myself."

"Don't be foolish, Alyssa. Think of that business loan hanging over your head. Doesn't that worry you?"

"I'd be lying if I said it didn't." In fact, it kept her awake nights. She swept her gaze over Cub from his dark hair to his tight jeans. Okay, it was one of the many things that kept her awake nights. She edged sideways to the door. "But I'll find a way to make my first loan payment without your intervention, thank you."

"*First* payment?" He lurched up from the bed, a disgusted grimace contorting his face for an instant. "You aren't even sure how to make the *first* payment?"

"There have been some…unforeseen circumstances, Cub." She grasped the doorknob, her muscles tightened from her fingers to her jaw. "With Shelby's new baby and me dealing with—my situation, we haven't made the contacts we'd hoped to this week.''

He staggered a step, then took two long strides to come up to her. His open hand thumped against the wall as he braced his arm straight a few inches from her shoulder. ''Not signing as many clients as you'd expected? What does that mean?''

The doorknob clattered in her palm. ''We haven't signed anyone.''

''But you will?''

''We have a couple prospects but they've expressed concern because we don't represent any big names.'' She studied the pattern on the carpet, so aware of his nearness, the aroma of his cologne, the subtle grating undertone to his damaged voice.

Pushing those aside, she concentrated on answering the question. ''I may have to go to Daddy to make the first loan payment, and you can just imagine how thrilled I'll be to do that.''

''Alyssa, I can—''

''No.'' She jerked her head up so fast the room seemed to do a half spin. When she caught Cub's intense gaze in the focus of her narrowed eyes, she said, ''I'll be beholden to my daddy as long as I live. That's the relationship we have. It's the relationship I always wanted to avoid with you.''

His smooth cheek ticked. ''You should have heard me out then.''

She struggled to control her breathing, which with Cub's closeness had grown shallow and quick. Her hand still on the doorknob, she lifted her chin, prepared to hear him out.

''What was it your partner said about me?'' he asked.

"You sure you want me to repeat it?" She managed a fairly earnest smile.

He grinned back, bending his arm so that his upper body came in even closer to hers. "He called me a hot property."

Hot. Yes, that fit. She used her free hand to swipe her hair off her suddenly warm neck.

"That Crowder fella also said I wasn't earning up to my potential without a good management team looking out for me."

"Cub, I don't think—" She clicked the door open and pulled it toward her.

"Alyssa, none of that meant a damned thing to me then, but now that I know about Jaycie, well, that's all changed. I can't rodeo forever, so I need to make the most of the time I have left, for the baby's sake."

She let the door fall closed but it did not latch. "What are you saying, Cub?"

"I'm saying I need someone to manage me and I'd like it to be you."

"Oh, Cub, I don't know what to say." Her heartbeat thudded in her ears, her thoughts and emotions a blur. "On one hand, your account alone could anchor our firm financially, provide us with prestige and—"

"Say yes, then."

*No.* That was pride talking. Mature, independent women did not make their business decisions on wounded pride. She needed him as a client. In fact, he'd probably hit on the only way in which she would accept help from this man, because they would be equals, helping each other.

Suddenly, all the pieces slid into place. For the first time ever, Cub had agreed to a true partnership, though she doubted he even realized that's just what he'd done. The perfection of it all made her spirits soar.

He inched in just a fraction closer. "C'mon, Alyssa, say yes to our working together."

"Yes."

"Yes?"

"Yes. Yes, yes, yes." She threw her arms around him. "Thank you, Cub, you won't regret this."

"I don't already."

The husky whisper tickled the shell of her ear, making her shiver. Her breasts met the hard wall of his chest as his arms closed around her to pull her to him.

"Cub, I—" The fine stubble on his jaw scraped at her cheek as she pulled her face away from his shoulder.

Their gazes fused.

"Say yes," he mouthed.

Her lips parted and before the word formed again, his mouth took hers.

How long had she dreamt of this? Of feeling his strong arms enclosing her, his body touching her inch for inch? Too long—and now that he had her in his embrace, his hungry mouth feasting on hers, she gave herself over to the sensation.

If joy were tactile this kiss was how it would feel. Explosive and yet so delicate she could notice every detail from the quiver of her own lips to the lingering sweetness of cotton candy on his tongue. She balled his shirtsleeve into her fist and moaned.

He slid his hand down her back to pull her hips against his own; even through their jeans she knew how badly he wanted her then. And if not for Jaycie—

"No, Cub, we can't—" She broke the kiss with a determined shove.

"I think we can." He reached for her again, unspeakable longing in his eyes.

"No, it will mess everything up. We can't afford that." She snatched at the doorknob and twisted it hard. "We have to get our priorities straight."

"Priorities?" He scowled his incomprehension.

"Yes." She caught her breath, exhaled hard, then met his gaze with cool clarity. "Jaycie comes first, then business."

"But what about us?" he whispered She felt the hurt reflected in his eyes, but she had to do the right thing, for their child's sake. "There is no 'us,' Cub. There just can't be."

She swung open the door and rushed out into the darkened hallway, his kiss and her declaration still humming on her lips.

# Chapter Seven

"What's this I hear about you coming back next season?" Price Wellman leaned both elbows back against the fence, his squinty-eyed gaze fixed on the flurry of rodeo activities around them.

The leather ties on his flashy rodeo chaps wrapped around Cub's fingers as he checked to make sure all was in readiness for his ride. "Where'd you hear that?"

"Some store-bought cowboy, name of Shelby Crowder, is spouting it all over." Price never looked at him. "Says he's your new manager."

He jerked the last tie tight. "Well, he ain't."

"I figured not."

"His partner is."

Cub scanned the arena to find the Cartwrights' VIP seats. The flash and glitter of Yip and Dolly standing and greeting passersby caught his attention, but the vision of Alyssa and Jaycie captured his heart.

He studied the baby girl he'd come to treasure in these last few days. Alyssa had been right about one thing—

their daughter wasn't exactly a sweet little angel. He chuckled over her stubbornness, her already clear-cut intention to have her way, her sparkling eyes, her impish dimple, her ready smile so like her mother's. He stole a glance at Alyssa, her face alight with love for their child.

It tore at his gut to know she might never look at him again with love in her eyes, that he might never hold her in his arms again, that there would be no other babies made between them. But then again…

He swiped the back of his hand over his lips. Her kiss had given him cause to hope. If he made this ride and the next and still had a leg to stand on—literally—then he'd go on to the Bull Riding World Finals and then the Grand Nationals in Vegas again. The endorsements and sponsorships he'd paid only half a mind to before would roll in and he'd make money for both of them. Another season of that and she'd be set in her business and maybe, just maybe, he'd have proven to her that he was a man to count on, a man worthy of her and their child. Provided the work didn't cripple him first.

"Then the rumors aren't true?"

"What rumors?" He swung his gaze to Price, feeling as if he'd just walked in on someone else's conversation.

"Them rumors 'bout you being so beat up another season would put you under the knife for sure, then facing a long rehab."

He grunted. "Oh, those rumors. Yep, they're true."

"Then why do this? Why promise another season?"

"You see that little bit of a red-haired thing in the stands?" He pointed to Jaycie standing on her mother's lap.

"Yep."

"That's why. Her mama won't take any real money

from me outright so I gotta let her earn it off my winnings and endorsements by managing me."

"Even if it kills you in the process?"

"What I got to live for if I ain't doing right by my only child, Price? Besides, it won't kill me, just bend me up a little." He slapped his friend on the back with a resounding whack.

"It'll wad you up in a little ball so we can roll you around in one of them fancy wheelchairs is what it'll do," Price muttered as Cub pushed off from the fence and headed away.

The last thing he saw before he went to the chute where his first ride of the night waited was Alyssa, with Jaycie in her lap. He lifted his hand to wave at them then realized they weren't looking his way. He let his hand drop. It felt heavy as his heart. Still, he memorized the picture his two girls made before he strode with purpose to get into position to make his ride.

Alyssa lapped one side of her sleek leather jacket over the other. The colors of the capacity crowd around them shimmered with movement. The crisp evening air brought a sharp tingle to her cheeks and the tip of her nose. Her fingers trembled as she locked down the brass zipper tab on Jaycie's fuzzy pink coat.

An old country-and-western tune twanged at top volume and high distortion through the speakers a few feet away from their seats. Yip tapped the silver-plated toe of his boot in time with the song. Dolly fidgeted in her seat, her jangling muffled tonight by her red-leather-and-fake-ponyskin coat, with more fringe on it than a flamenco dancer's shawl.

Despite it all, Alyssa had to smile at her parents. She loved the pair of show-offs and while they had given her an unconventional and sometimes frustrating childhood, they loved her, too. As Yip would put it, they loved her more than their very next breath.

Before she had Jaycie, she had no idea the depth of that kind of love. Sure, she'd loved Cub, loved him in a way she believed few people ever got to really experience, because she loved him for what he was, not what he could be, or what she'd wanted him to be. If only he could have returned that love in kind, she thought, everything would have been so different. But he didn't even know the real Alyssa, didn't try to get to know her—how could he have loved her?

She hugged Jaycie close. The important thing, she told herself, wasn't how she loved Cub or *if* he had loved her but that they both loved their child. Just as she had reminded herself during her hot, memorable kiss with Cub, the baby was their first priority. No matter how he made her feel, no matter how she thought he felt about her, she knew she could never show how much she cared about Cub again.

"Next up, a rider we've all been waiting to see." The voice of the first of the pair of rodeo announcers boomed so loud it shook the seats beneath them.

Alyssa craned her neck for the best possible view.

"He's been absent from Summit City for the last two years, Vernon," the second announcer chimed in. "His draw tonight, Bowdlerizer, has dumped many a cowboy this season and given quite a few winning rides as well. Should be a good ride."

"Count on that, Earl Junior," the announcer named Vernon said back. "But it's this young man's second ride tonight that's really got his fans excited. In the fourth of five rides this season, as part of a spectacular promotional event, Cub Goodacre will take on Diablo's Heartbreak."

The crowd around them cheered.

"But first Cub's got to concentrate on this ride," Earl Junior explained. "He's a champion, ladies and gentlemen, and he takes every ride just as seriously as he does his personal duel with Diablo's Heartbreak."

Alyssa tried not to listen but the announcers went on relentlessly about Cub.

"You got that right, Earl Junior. Any time a man climbs on one of these bulls, he's sittin' dead on top of a ton of danger."

"And that's why they earn the big money, and—Okay, now, looks like he's got his mount, we're just waiting for him to give his sign."

Alyssa pressed her lips together. She dug her fingers into the fuzzy pile of her daughter's coat and scooted to the edge of her seat.

"And that's it," Vernon said, keeping a steady tone. "He's given the sign he's ready. I want y'all to give a big Summit City welcome to Cub Goodacre!"

The chute burst open. The crowd roared.

Alyssa drew a stinging breath of autumn air and—shut her eyes so tight they burned.

Eight seconds. How could such a fleeting measure of time seem to take forever to pass?

*One Mississippi, two Mississippi.* She tried counting down the time, but the thudding hoofbeats of the bull, the blaring comments of the announcers, the rumblings of the crowd all begged for her attention.

"Please don't get hurt," she murmured into the nubby fabric of Jaycie's hood. "Please just hang on and—"

And obnoxious air horn blasted through her sightless plea.

"Hee-haw! He done it!"

She slowly opened her eyes to find her parents standing, cheering Cub's accomplishment.

"What a ride, folks. What a ride!" The announcers rattled off stats and opinions.

Nothing else registered in Alyssa's mind except the sight of Cub, favoring one leg but otherwise unhurt, climbing the fence while the bullfighters, dressed in colorful clown outfits and makeup, drew Bowdlerizer's attention away from his rider. She sighed and swallowed, ignoring the dampness rimming her lashes. He did it. Cub was safe—for now.

"Hee-haw!" Jaycie clapped and stamped her foot on Alyssa's thigh.

Yip reached out to swing the child up into his arms. "He did good, your daddy did, gal. Didn't he, Alyssa?"

"I wasn't watching," she admitted. "But judging from the response, I'd said he did fine. That's definitely good for business."

Yip snorted like a hog at the dinner trough. "Yeah, and your interest in that cowboy is all business, I suppose?"

"Yes. Yes, it is, purely business." She angled her chin up and met her father's steady gaze with one of her own.

"Bit of advice, sweetheart."

"What?" She tossed back her hair.

"Next time you try to convince me you don't give a horse's hindquarters about the man, best you wipe the tears of worried affection from your eyes first." His big, rough finger swept away the damp bead from the corner of her eye with startling gentleness.

"Excuse me, Daddy." She sniffled but did not acknowledge her own unshed tears. "If you and Mama don't mind watching Jaycie, I'd like to go check on Cub.''

Her daddy didn't say a word, but then again, he didn't have to.

"I'm doing it as his manager, Daddy.'' The explanation rushed out in ready defense. "It's part of my job to watch over my client, to make sure he's in top condition to make that big ride.''

"You do that, gal.'' He nodded his head, his eyes twinkling. "You go right ahead and check on your *client*.''


"Hey, Alyssa, thanks for coming down to see me.'' Cub swatted at the seat of his jeans, not because he gave a damn about the dust there, but because he didn't want to appear too anxious over Alyssa's response.

"You know that's part of my job, Cub.'' She paused beside him in a dimly lit hallway reserved for cowboys and people with the proper passes.

The narrow passage forced them into close quarters, so close he could hear the squeak of her athletic shoes on the smooth concrete, smell the night air in her hair mingling with the musky leather of her coat. The thick fringe of his chaps dangled against the pale blue denim over her thigh when he stood straight again. If they were any closer, he wouldn't trust himself not to kiss her.

He drew off his hat and occupied himself with checking it over as he asked, "So, what did you think of the ride?''

"The crowd loves you.''

It was foolhardy to want her approval, but he did. He lowered the hat in one hand to his side, lifted his head and searched her hazel eyes. "I didn't ask about the crowd.''

"I..." She pressed her lips into a tight line. Her breasts lifted with a deep breath, which she held so long he wanted to believe she meant it as an offering.

He raised his open hand.

"I have to confess, I didn't watch your ride." She exhaled.

He touched one finger to the ID badge clipped to her collar. "Too busy using your access pass to solicit other cowboys?"

"You know better than that," she said in a clipped whisper.

He did. He'd said it just to rile her, just to get some kind of response besides evasiveness from the woman's lips. And he wasn't about to stop now. "Then, tell me, how is it you happen to miss the night's first ride by your one and only...hot property?"

"I was nervous, okay?" She pushed his hand from her badge.

He hoped she'd deny he was just a piece of property to her.

He placed his hat back on his head, letting the brim shadow his eyes from hers, and waited for her to say more.

"I..." She shut her eyes and swallowed, then looked at the floor. "I couldn't watch."

"You *couldn't?*"

"No, I *couldn't.*" She jerked her head up.

From the darkness beneath his custom hat brim, he sought more from her eyes than her words revealed. Could she not watch because she cared too much? Forget about *too much,* if she gave one damned hoot what happened to his sorry hide, he'd take that. Take it and cherish it, and hope—

"I couldn't watch, Cub, because I have so much at stake here."

"Go on."

"Well, you know the business. You being my highest profile client, my *only* client. If you were disqualified—"

The woman could insult his maturity. She could reject his advances. He'd take that like a man. What he would not do, however, was stand there and let her belittle the only thing he did well, the only thing he'd have left besides their daughter if Alyssa had her way.

"I don't get disqualified," he said through his clenched jaw. "Thrown halfway to heaven on a hell of a ride, maybe, but not disqualified."

"Or worse," she finished her sentence.

"Yeah, well, I don't expect the worst when I ride, and as my manager—as the mother of my child—I don't think you should either." He felt ashamed for talking to her like that, yet his pain drove him to it.

"Cub, I—"

"I got to go get ready for my next ride." He pushed past her, afraid of what else he might say and later regret. At the end of the hallway, he turned and pointed his finger back at her small, dark figure. "This time, keep your eyes open, Alyssa. You'll see just what your *husband* is capable of. Then maybe, just once, you'll feel proud of your man, not mad cause he didn't give you the kind of marriage you dreamed you'd have, or afraid because you banked your business on him."

"Cub, I'm not—"

"I swear to you, Alyssa, this time I will not let you down."

# Chapter Eight

"Nicknamed Cub by his first rodeo partners, Jacob Goodacre is a world-class bull rider, just the kind Diablo's Heartbreak loves to take down a notch." Vernon's voice echoed through the arena. "Heartbreak, as the cowboys call him, makes his best trips when he knows a champion is on his back."

"That's the mark of good rough stock animals," Earl Junior added. "But this two thousand pounds of contrary beef takes it one further—he seems to know when Cub in particular has cowboyed up."

"And he ain't one bit happy about it, neither."

"The feeling is mutual, Vernon." Earl Junior chuckled amicably into the open mike. "The idea for this promotional event started last season when Heartbreak gave Cub an especially nasty wreck. Afterward Cub told everyone, 'This ain't just professional anymore, it's personal.'"

"And so the challenge was on, with big-time sponsorship, Cub agreed to meet Heartbreak five times this year to see who was truly the best. So far, Cub is ahead two rides to one. Tonight could either move him ahead or tie it up.''

"Either way, they'll meet again in six weeks in New Mexico for the final ride, Vernon.''

"That's right, Earl Junior. No one knows if that final ride will be a showdown for bragging rights as the best on the circuit or the last roundup for one that's already lost the show.''

"Tonight's ride will decide.''

Cub lowered himself into the narrow chute with calculated caution.

"I watched a replay of your last exhibition ride on this critter.'' Price leaned in to talk to Cub as he prepared for the ride. "He may blow out of the chute, like always, but you gotta be ready to hang on like a virgin to her virtue if he starts to spin.''

Cub nodded. In the bad wreck that Heartbreak gave him, the bull had spun to the left and Cub hadn't compensated quickly enough. He knew the danger involved, firsthand.

"What a thrill it is to be able to witness a ride like this tonight, folks,'' Earl Junior drawled over the loudspeakers as they waited for Cub's signal. "Cub Goodacre and Diablo's Heartbreak seem perfectly matched in temperament and skill.''

"That's what you think,'' Cub muttered in response to the announcer's assessment. "We're damn *near* matched, you and me, fella.'' He warily focused on the familiar sight of the bull he'd ridden time and again this season. He worked his gloved fingers under the rosin-covered bull rope, then pounded the sticky, hand-plaited rope into his open palm. It pulled taut around the animal snorting beneath him. "But I got one thing on you, *Heartbreak*—"

Cub gritted his teeth, visually checking his position as well as using all his senses to make sure he was properly placed and ready.

"I been riding my own brand of heartbreak for a long time now," he told the animal, as a means of psyching himself up for the task ahead. "And I've always mastered it."

Cub looked up and caught a glimpse of Alyssa in the stands.

Her eyes found him, then quickly darted away.

"It don't look like that's going to change now." Cub crunched his hat down hard on his head. He took deep breath and gave the sign. "Let's rock and roll, you ornery old son of a—"

"Which will it be, man or—" Vernon's words were cut off as Diablo's Heartbreak blew out of the chute.

The crowd roared.

Cub dug his heels in, his hand high, his body over his grip as it should be.

He'd heard a man tell once of the Zen of bull riding, of the mental demands, of the necessity of the cowboy to be "at one" with the bull. Cub didn't know a hang about the particulars of that philosophy, but at this very moment, he knew he wasn't achieving it.

Heartbreak's hooves exploded in the dust like lightning striking driftwood dead-on.

Every bone and joint and muscle in Cub's body screamed out at the jolt. He wasn't riding that bull, he realized, the bull was toying with him like a kid with a punchball, and the blasted animal was about to take his new toy for a hellwind whirl.

*Hang on like a virgin to her virtue if he starts to spin.* Price's advice came back in a flash.

Heartbreak snorted hot breath and made sounds that would scare the devil himself. He hooked his horns hard and high like some demon crowing out his certain victory.

Cub hung on and set himself for a merciless twist left.

Then Heartbreak thrashed his mighty body into a spin, to the *right.*

The pain in Cub's hip split through him, sending fiery shards tearing downward through his knee to his ankle. Deep but dull, the pain in his upper body doubled him forward. In that instant of blinding agony, his hand shot out to his side, seeking by instinct to grab at his injured hip.

*Thrown but never disqualified.* That's the promise he'd made to Alyssa and it fought its way into his thoughts through his impossible torment. His hand clenched the air and did not touch his body, which had now gone so numb he saw rather than felt himself being hurled from the bull's back.

As Cub landed, first shoulder, then chest, then chin in the dirt, the eight-second blow horn sounded. It was the last thing he heard before sinking into oblivious darkness.

"Cub? Can you hear me, Cub?"

From somewhere in the far-off distance, Cub heard the voice of his friend, Price. He wanted to call back but had no voice, no body for that matter. His mind had wakened in a lifeless form, one he could not control.

Out of pure instinct, he gulped air into his stifled lungs and coughed it back out. Slowly, as if his body were just now catching up to his brain, his physical senses came swirling back to him.

First he smelled the blood and mud caked around his nose, then he tasted it on his swollen lip. He heard the hushed tones of concern swimming around him and realized he was lying on a hard, cold table of some kind. Then the first wave of pain hit.

"I can't stand this, Price. How is he? Is he alive?" asked a female voice that sounded as if it came from inside a well.

"I don't know, I'll ask him." Price's voice rang clear as if he stood directly overhead.

Every inch of Cub's body throbbed except for a patch on his scalp and his left eye, which he opened with extreme care to find his friend peering down at him.

"You alive?" Price asked.

"I'd better be," Cub managed to grumble. "'Cause if I'm not, I'm looking into the face of one butt-ugly angel."

"It's okay, Alyssa," Price called over his shoulder. "He's alive, awake and his sweet ol' cuddly self."

"Cub? We're in the emergency tent at the arena. You got knocked out cold for a couple minutes. Do you know who I am?" Alyssa's face filled his hazy view.

"It's all ...so...foggy," he murmured. "Come closer."

She leaned in over him.

He eased his right eye open just enough to confirm the genuine worry in her face. The caring ran so deep in her searching gaze it reached beyond the physical and emotional pain and told him what he had always longed to know. Alyssa still loved him.

And he had let her down—again.

A temporary failing, he told himself. He'd ride again

and win again and make her proud, not to mention keep her business solvent.

"Cub?"

He felt her breath on his cheek.

"You do recognize me, don't you?" she asked.

"Yeah." He reached up to flutter his fingers through her soft hair. "You're my wife."

She smiled.

"I'm going to send the doc back in here," Price told them both. "Maybe now he can do something more for the pain."

Cub grunted a response to that as his hand fell back to his side. Alyssa's smile did him more good than anything available to modern medicine.

And he had let her down, the accusation echoed again through his mind.

"Alyssa, I'm sorry I—"

"Sorry? About what?" She swept her cool fingertips along his left temple.

"Well, that less than spectacular ride wasn't exactly—" He shut his eyes. "Good for business."

"Who gives a hoot about business right now, Cub?" She set herself on the edge of the table where he lay. "The main thing is that you're all right."

She did still care; the realization pounded through his body with every heartbeat. She still cared and he'd screwed things up for her today real good. Didn't it just figure?

"Besides, you're wrong, Cub."

"What?" He winced and forced both eyes fully open. "Wrong about what?"

"About business. From a purely business point of view your little stunt tonight was golden." She brushed some dirt from his shoulder and he didn't even mind the pain it caused. "Not that I'd want you to have done it on purpose, of course, but since it happened this way—"

He blinked. "Maybe I ain't got a world of business sense and maybe tonight's fall on my head didn't improve that none, but as far as I understand, you're talking nonsense, gal. How can getting thrown be a good thing?"

"Are you joking? It's fabulous, Cub." A light shone in her eyes as she spoke in hushed enthusiasm. "Don't you see? It ups the ante. Now that you and Diablo's Heartbreak are tied, the final showdown is winner-take-all."

He groaned at the very thought of another ride.

"It's like something out of a movie," she went on. "From a management position, it's like winning the lottery."

"Next time can we just do one of those scratch-and-win tickets?"

She laughed. "Tonight's ride has given me something I can parlay into all kinds of endorsements and personal appearances and who knows what all."

"I see." So he hadn't let her down—not yet. He still had one more crack at proving himself and providing for her. "You want to create a big buildup for the next time I meet up with that damned ornery bull."

"There won't be a next time, Cub, not if I have anything to say about it." The rodeo doctor, a round-faced, bearded fellow Cub had known for years, strode into the tent.

"Lucky for me, I don't take orders from a man too tall to straddle a bull, too bowlegged to ride a bronc without slippin' off and too mean to work on livestock so they let him torment cowboys instead." Cub forced himself up on one elbow, determined to seem more fit that he felt. "Howdy, Doc."

"Cub," Doc nodded. "Looks like you tried to waltz left when your partner went right."

"It happens."

"Doc, what did you mean when you said 'there won't be a next time'?" Alyssa touched the doctor's sleeve.

A new shade colored her expression now, one that made Cub's aching stomach muscles clench and burn. If Doc blurted out the whole ugly truth, Alyssa's excitement, concern and the faint hint of love would fade to fear, disappointment and, worst of all, pity.

"Doc meant he's going to give me some pointers so next time Heartbreak won't dump me," Cub said with wry sarcasm, hoping Doc would take the hint and shut up.

"I mean I've checked this cowboy out," he told Alyssa before turning to Cub. "You should have walked away from that dusting. But you didn't and I couldn't figure why not—until I had a little talk with Price about your old injury."

"You mean his bruised hip," Alyssa volunteered before Cub could deny it.

"That's just what he means." Cub found it darn near impossible to draw a threatening bead on the doctor with one eye almost swelled shut.

"Bruised hip?" He mirrored Cub's drunken-eyed stare back at him. "That what they call it?"

Cub said nothing.

Doc stroked his beard. "Makes sense now. Lots of cowboys in their prime do get waylaid by a...*bruise*."

Cub shut his eyes and let his head fall back.

"A bruised ego, maybe," Doc muttered. "One that won't let them admit the truth."

"What truth?" Alyssa asked the doctor.

He didn't respond.

"What truth?" she demanded of Cub, tugging at his shirtsleeve to force the issue.

"The truth is, Alyssa." He didn't look at her as he spoke. "I hurt myself bad, but I have crack sports-medicine specialists working for me, and with their help, I'll be up and around, ready to meet up with Heartbreak in New Mexico in six weeks."

"Sports medicine or voodoo witch doctor, Cub, they can only do so much." Doc sneered and moved in close to tell him with quiet conviction, "If it were up to me, I'd ban you from ever again mounting anything uglier than yourself."

Cub met that conviction with steel of his own. "That only rules out a handful of bulls on the circuit, Doc, and just about half of the women who'd date you."

Doc drew away and muttered a curse, shaking his head as he turned to get something from the workspace behind them.

"Cub!" Alyssa shifted into the spot where Doc had stood. "That was not a very nice thing to say."

"I'm kidding him, Alyssa." He pushed himself upright, then paused, unable to swing his legs off the table yet. "Doc kidded me about not riding again and I came back in kind, that's what guys do."

"Cub, I don't think he was—"

"Here you go." Doc thrust a white piece of paper at Cub. "This will help you handle the pain until you can get in touch with those specialists you're so fond of."

Cub gripped the icy edge of the metal examining table. "I don't need—"

"Take it." The paper crackled in his hand. He twisted his head to speak to Alyssa. "And he probably ought to have someone looking after him, at least for a few days.''

"I can do that,'' Alyssa assured him in a short, breathy voice. She turned to face Cub. "If you don't mind staying out at the ranch with me...''

Yesterday he'd have taken her up on that like a calf mothering up for its first feeding, just for the chance to be near her and the baby. But now— He could not look into her eyes, knowing he would see how much she had already begun to feel sorry for him.

"It's either that or have Price move into your hotel room to make sure you don't fall and bust your pretty pug nose, Goodacre,'' Doc warned.

Having a friend move in to take care of him made him seem even more of an invalid, Cub decided. At least if he was at the ranch he'd have some chance to show Alyssa that he wasn't done in.

Cub snatched the prescription from Doc's hand, avoided the dirt-eating grin on the man's face and said in a reluctant grumble, "Well, I don't need no nurse-maid, but I guess when you put it that way, I'll choose going to the ranch.''

"You'll be up and around in no time, Cub.'' Alyssa struggled to plop the suitcase brought from his hotel onto the chest of drawers. The fact that Cub didn't even raise his voice to offer help told her that the pain medication had started to take effect.

"No time, darlin','' he echoed in a groggy whisper.

She watched him in the huge, framed mirror as he eased himself onto the bed and back against the pillows she had plumped for him, not bothering to lift his legs onto the mattress. She'd never seen the man so weary, so vulnerable, so…human before. The sight warmed her in ways she could not have expected.

Cub was back, just as she'd wished in her letter. But now that he was here, so in need of her, it wasn't good-bye she had on her mind. The suitcase latches sprang open with a pop when she flicked them with her thumbs.

"I'll just put your things in the top drawer for now. You can sort them out for yourself later."

He hummed some kind of reply, his hat dipped low to shadow his eyes.

She lifted the top of the case and looked inside. The subtle scent reminded her of Cub. She drew the smell in deep and held her breath a moment. A quiver worked through the pit of her stomach as she reached inside to touch his things for the first time in so long, too long. Her fingers sank into the soft fabric of a black T-shirt; her gaze scanned the neatly packed shaving things, the two gray boxes that surely held his latest or favorite championship belt buckles, a yellow paper folded so she could plainly see Jaycie's picture on the battered flyer.

That touched her more than any other thing she saw and it filled her with guilt.

"You know, I can get you some real pictures of Jaycie to carry." She twisted her head to make herself heard above the sound of pulling the top drawer open.

"That'd be nice," he laid his hand on his side and shifted his body stiffly. "I'd like that."

With his shirt in her hand, Alyssa waited and watched Cub try to make himself comfortable at his odd angle across the pillows. She couldn't help but think of Doc's concern, which only added to her own. Something was very wrong with Cub and she intended to find out just what it was, not because it threatened her business deal with him, but because…

He was the father of her child. She felt displaced maternal instincts for the wounded little boy in him. She hated to see anyone in pain. None of her old excuses for her disturbing feelings held water. The old defenses just would not work anymore and it was time she admitted it.

She had known she would always love Cub, but she had thought she had grown beyond wishing they could work it out. Now, as she studied him trying to rest on the bed in the room directly across the hall from her own, she knew. Having Cub here was not a strategic business move. It was a last-ditch effort to try to make a connection, to find if she could form a real partnership with this man suddenly humbled just enough to give her hope.

"I wish you'd trusted me enough to tell me how badly you were hurt, Cub," she said softly.

"Not a matter of trust, Alyssa, it's a matter of truth. I just ain't hurt that bad." She couldn't see his eyes but his smooth cheek flinched to belie his remark.

"Truth?" She dropped his shirt into the open drawer. "You wouldn't know the truth if it bit you on the butt."

"You calling me a liar?" Amusement, not challenge, colored his tone.

"I'm just saying that your head may still be as thick as a bull's skull." She tossed his shaving kit in with a clatter. "But maybe it's time you admitted the rest of you just isn't that tough."

"Wanna bet?"

"What I want—" She spun around to see him grappling with his own body to bring his legs up onto the bed.

The grimace of exertion on his pale lips made her

gasp. Then she realized that if they were ever going to work together as equals, this was where it would begin.

"Here, let me help you." She took two long strides toward the bed.

"I can do just fine by myself."

"Cub Goodacre, don't you snarl at me like some bad-tempered hound dog." She placed her hands on her hips. "Besides, weren't you the one who told me that a person shouldn't be ashamed to ask for help when they need it?"

"*If* they need it." He leaned forward, his hat still shading his eyes from her.

"Which you do." She stepped forward again and reached out to whisk his hat from his head. Darned if she'd let him hide from her while she attempted to get through to him.

She settled the hat on the nightstand beside him, realizing only after she did how close this brought her to Cub. The warmth from his body rose to envelop her. She swept back her hair and met his gaze.

"Please, Cub," she whispered. "Let me help you."

He set his jaw.

For an instant, she thought his stubborn pride would win out again. Then something flickered in the depths of his eyes, and a crooked smile eased across his lips.

"Okay, darlin', you can help me—"

Help him what? Her teeth sank into her lower lip as all manner of possibilities flashed through her mind, most of them vivid enough to bring sudden heat to her chest and cheeks.

"You can help me," he said again, "get these darned boots off."

"What—? Oh, of course." It wasn't what she'd expected. It wasn't what she'd fantasized. But it was a start.

Alyssa bent and grabbed his boot by the heel.

"Not like that," he howled.

"Why?" She froze. "Did I hurt you?"

"Now that that painkiller kicked in, Heartbreak himself couldn't hurt me if he sat square on me." He laughed.

"Why'd you stop me then?"

"Because you know the proper way to help a cowboy off with his boots." He made a circle with his finger.

"Oh, for—" She turned around, straddling his leg and bending over so he could prop one foot on her backside as she worked lose his boot. "You just want me to do it this way so I can't see if you're really hurting more than you let on."

"That ain't the only reason," he growled.

His first boot dropped to the floor with a thud and he moved the freed foot to flex against her rear.

"Cub." A giggle bubbled up from her throat. "You're in no condition to—"

"Wanna bet on that, too?" His second boot bumped against the sculpted carpet just as his hand closed over her hip.

In one quick tumble she fell backward onto the bed, her legs tangled with Cub's.

"Cub, we can't."

"We *could*—if we really wanted to." He pulled her on top of him. "At least, I think I still remember how."

The husky longing in his tone rasped against prickling nerves. Her skin tingled with the need to feel his touch. Her body sought to stretch beside his, meeting hard muscle with yielding flesh.

On instinct, her thighs parted, her knees settling on

the bed to hold her body just off his straining hips. A new yearning stirred deep within her.

Was this how they would mend the rift? She closed her eyes and tried to think of her goal, to begin again with a true partnership. Was this giving too much too soon? Or was she showing him her strength by taking an equal role in something they both wanted so badly?

Cub groaned and reached for her as she kneeled above him. He cupped her breasts with hands so callused she could feel their roughness beneath the thin material of her shirt.

Goals and roles, and second-guessing what she should do, slipped away as she gave herself to the sensation.

He stroked the aching center of her breasts with his thumb.

She threw her head back and shut her eyes. "Oh, yes."

Closer, she wanted to be closer. She lowered her chin to find his gaze. Her back straight, she pushed her hips down to meet his.

He groaned, his teeth clenched. The look on his face chased away every spark of desire his touch had rekindled.

"Cub?" She swung her leg off him. "Oh, my gosh, Cub, you are really, really hurt."

He blew out a hard puff of air but said nothing, his eyes clenched tightly shut.

Her hands on his face, she leaned in close. "Why didn't you tell me it was this bad?"

"It's...not." He hardly had the breath to force the words through.

"Damn it, Cub." She slapped at his chest and pulled away. "Stop trying to protect me. What do you think?

That if you show even a little human weakness, you can't be a good father, a good husband?''

He opened his eyes, his pain subsided. "Let me show you just how good a husband I can be."

"Just stop it." She pushed up from the bed.

"Alyssa, don't make such a big deal out of this. So, I'm a little bruised—''

"Oh!" She threw her hands up, then strode to the door. She yanked it open, swallowed hard to keep from speaking so loud it drew her parents' attention and said, "I thought there was a chance we could work things through, but if you're going to lie to me, I just don't see how that can happen."

She slammed the door behind her. So much for a partnership, she decided. Now it was time to give Mr. Take-Charge a taste of his own medicine.

# Chapter Nine

"Cub Goodacre hostage situation, day twenty-one." Cub leaned forward at the kitchen table to hand Jaycie her tippy cup filled with milk. "Today my keeper promises to take me out, but she refuses to tell me where. If I don't come back, Jaycie, I want you to have my hat."

"Very funny." Alyssa leaned her hip against the kitchen counter and swirled rich-smelling coffee under her nose. She took a tentative sip from her cup.

Jaycie clapped her hands together, her sparkling eyes fixed on Cub. She pointed one chubby finger at him. "Funny."

He pointed to himself. "Daddy."

"She had it right the first time." Alyssa smiled at their daughter. "Now eat your breakfast, both of you, I have a big day planned."

Cub slumped back in his chair. Three weeks he'd been at this ranch. It felt like three years. But judging from the progress he'd made with his child, his wife and his rehabilitation, it might as well have been three days.

After their one flash of passion, Alyssa had become all business again. Though he felt the old fires building every time she helped him with his physical therapy, and saw in her eyes that she felt it, too, she always stayed outwardly cool and in control. At least, he took small comfort in telling himself, she hadn't felt sorry for him. She'd proved that with her taskmaster attitude toward his exercise and her creative approaches to managing what was left of his career.

He thought of the endorsements she'd found for him. He appreciated the work on her part, but the new contracts hardly represented the kind of money he'd bring after he bested Diablo's Heartbreak in New Mexico. Alyssa didn't see it that way, of course; she wanted to press on, finding other ways to promote him in case his last ride never happened.

But it would happen. The specialists felt confident it would. And more important, Cub *knew* it would. It had to, as much for Alyssa and Jaycie's sake now as for his own. That's why he'd taken no chances making the arrangements for it and the increased publicity and sponsorship that ride could bring.

He felt a twinge of guilt over going behind Alyssa's back and dealing with her glad-handling hustler of a partner. Frankly, for the kind of money Cub needed to make in the next few weeks, he needed a hustler. He pushed the rolled cuff of his sleeve into the crook of his elbow as he recalled the hushed phone conversations with Crowder taken on the private line in his room.

It spoke volumes of the new opinion Yip and Dolly had of him that they had not only let him move into the ranch to mend, but had installed the second phone line and provided an answering machine so Cub could conduct business.

Never underestimate the power of a few championships and a shared interest in spoiling a certain girl baby to bring folks together, he thought. While his relationship with his in-laws had improved considerably, it was the relationship with Alyssa that stayed uppermost in his mind.

If he could just get her to admit where he stood with her, that would help. Even if she still wanted the divorce, at least he'd know. But she was too quick with her defenses, and too smart to let him see her hand until she was ready, not at all the guileless young woman he had married. He admired that change in her as much as it frustrated him.

"Your mama treats me more like another kid than like your daddy," he joked to the toddler poking cereal circles into her mouth.

Jaycie pointed at him again. "Funny."

Cub's fork scritched against his plate as he scraped it back and forth to break the yolk of his fried egg. Like mother, like daughter, he thought. Until Alyssa fully made up her mind about him he didn't see how or why Jaycie would either.

He frowned at having his other sore spot exposed by his daughter. "I don't know why she can't just say it. Why can't she just once call me Daddy?"

"She will, Cub, give her time."

He pushed his plate away, his appetite gone. "I don't have time."

"Why?" She took another sip of coffee, arching an eyebrow at him from over the cup. "You think you're going somewhere?"

He braced his forearms against the edge of the table and angled his shoulders forward, speaking in precise yet intensely personal tone. "You think I'm *not* going somewhere?"

Her gaze flickered downward.

He pressed his point. "Because if in all the big plans you've laid out for me while I've been stove up, you've decided I'm stayin' on here, darlin', it's something I'd like to know about."

"I never…I mean, I don't…" She set her coffee cup on the counter with a definite thunk, crossed her arms, sighed and scowled at him.

Jaycie mimicked her mother down to the letter, clunking down her tippy cup, crossing her arms and puffing her cheeks out around a pouting frown. Like mother, like daughter.

Alyssa shook her hair back. "Let's just deal with things as they come, Cub. You know my daddy always says, 'don't borrow trouble.'"

Jaycie wobbled her head, making one or two of her fluffy red curls waft from side to side.

"She means don't *marry* trouble," he corrected, speaking to their baby in hopes of raising a smile.

"Oh, yeah, Daddy really thinks you're a lot of trouble." Alyssa's laughter rang genuine, but was tipped with calm detachment. "Mama, too. Since you've been here they've only treated you like the king of the cowboys."

He brushed one finger over his child's plump cheek. "Guess that makes you a princess, Jaycie."

"Pwincess." She patted her tummy.

"And since your mama won't let me buy you a p-o-n-y—" He spelled the word because he knew saying it would set off both these females and he'd be the target of their anger. Not the kind of reaction he wanted while he tried to find an acceptable footing with them both.

"Maybe she will let me get you a pretty pink cowgirl hat—maybe with one of those rhinestone jobs, you know, like the rodeo queens wear?"

He waggled his fingers over his head to better illustrate.

Jaycie wriggled her own fingers over her head. "Me hat. Mine."

"Oh, please, don't go putting those kinds of ideas into her head." This time her laughter warmed the brittle air around them.

"I don't see why not." He touched Jaycie's nose. "Every baby girl should be her daddy's little princess. I'm sure you were."

"Yes, that's true." She sighed.

"And still are."

"Hold it right there, Cub, I see where this is headed."

"You do?" He blinked, his mind scrambling to figure out what she meant.

"I am no one's little princess, cowboy. And neither is Jaycie." She walked over and pulled Jaycie from her booster seat at the table. "We don't need the protection and guidance of some lord and master, however benevolent. I am not like your old lover and I am not like your mother. If left to my own judgment, I won't make a mess of things, no matter what you or my daddy thinks."

He didn't doubt that a moment, but before he could tell her so, she rushed on.

"I won't raise my daughter with that kind of thinking." Hoisting the little girl high against her, she tipped her chin up. "I want her to know that we can take care of ourselves."

Jaycie's rounded chin lifted, too.

Cub folded his arms on the tabletop. He'd wondered

where he stood with the two of them, and it seemed he had his answer—he stood on the outside of their family circle.

"Now, if you'll finish your breakfast, we have an appointment to make." Alyssa turned on her heel.

"Yes, ma'am," he grumbled in deadpan sarcasm, glowering at the eggs gone cold on his plate.

"Me pwincess. Him's funny."

Cub jerked his head up to see Jaycie, her arms stretched out toward him over Alyssa's shoulder.

He scooted his chair back. "I think she wants to stay with me."

"She's just jabbering," Alyssa snapped.

"The baby want pwincess funny."

He stood without much more than a twinge of pain in his hip. "Sounds pretty clear to me. Let her stay."

Alyssa's whole back went rigid.

"I'll even let her feed herself, no pushy lord-and-master stuff, I promise." He grinned and winked at the baby struggling to reach for him.

"Oh, all right." She turned and settled the child into her seat without so much as a glance at Cub. "I'll be back in half an hour and I want you both fed and cleaned up so we can get going."

"You're the boss." He raised his open hands in a gesture of sincere submission.

That made her look at him. Her dark lashes fluttered as though she were seeing something for the first time. She tucked her hair behind her ear. "Okay, well, I'll be back."

"We'll be fine."

She stopped mid-nod to study him a moment, her lips almost quirked into a half smile, then she finished the nod, turned and walked out.

"Is it just my imagination or did I just score some points with her?" He handed the baby a piece of cereal.

Jaycie popped the food into her mouth and giggled.

"Well, at least I know I've made some headway with you, sweet thing." He cupped his hand over the downy curls on her head. "Now we got to work on your mama."

Jaycie stabbed her finger up toward his face. "Him's pwincess funny."

"Yeah, we got to work on that, too."


"Alyssa, darlin', have you lost your ever-lovin' mind?"

The wind whipped a lock of pale red hair across the bridge of Alyssa's nose, but that did not veil the view of Cub's astonished expression. She drew in the cool morning air and blew it out her rounded lips. This was it, she told herself. This moment would gel their professional relationship and hopefully provide a glimmer of insight as to the potential for them as a couple.

"I assure you, Cub, I haven't lost anything—yet. Unless, of course, this is your way of telling me I've lost you as a client?"

"No," he grumbled.

He glanced up at the banner plastered against the empty barn on the piece of land bordering Price Wellman's property. The morning sun stung Alyssa's eyes but his remained shaded by his trusty—and far too sexy-looking for her well-being—hat.

"Cub Goodacre's School of Bull Riding," he read.

"Kinda grows on you, huh?"

He leaned on his cane with one hand. "More like it sticks to you, like something you step on in a pasture."

"So, you're saying my idea stinks? You hate it." She

expected him to hate it. In fact, she had planned for him to hate it, or at least hate the idea of her having set it up without his input. She just wanted him to see how it felt for someone else to take charge of your life, your finances, your future; only then could he understand and appreciate the importance of a real partnership.

"Well, I wouldn't exactly say I hate it—"

"Go on," she urged. "Say you hate it. You won't hurt my feelings, honest."

He huffed out a deep sigh. "Okay. It's true. I hate it."

"Too bad. It's a done deal."

"A what?" He pushed his hat to the back of his head.

"Acting as your manager, I've made all the arrangements." She braced herself for whatever response came her way, glad that Cub had suggested they let Price and his wife take Jaycie on a short ride around the property to give them privacy if only for a few minutes. "It's all in your best interest, of course. I'm only looking out for you as a *manager* should, to keep you from making any mistakes or bad decisions on your own."

The morning sun glinted along the length of his broad shoulders as he folded his arms. "In other words, 'gotcha.'"

She blinked in feigned innocence. "Why, Cub, I don't know what you mean."

"Like heck you don't." He smiled.

That small gesture, combined with the sight of him in a fitted western shirt and jeans faded and worn just enough to mold over his narrow bull rider's butt and powerful thighs, made her shiver.

"You think I don't know that your little cakewalk on a canyon ridge here was meant to make a point?"

"Did it work?"

"No."

Of course not. What was she thinking when she expected to make a dent in that bull-hide exterior of his?

"It didn't work, darlin', because it was a case of closing the barn door after the mule had already got out."

She raised her eyebrows. "And just who is the mule in his case?"

He raised one hand as if taking an oath. "Slap a yoke on my neck and call me Francis. I been stubborn as a mule and twice as ornery."

"Cub, I don't know what to say…"

"I was wrong to make those decisions for the both of us, Alyssa. Being beholden to you these last few weeks, seeing how much you're capable of doing, it all just shows me how much I shortchanged you, shortchanged us both."

Did he mean that? His expression seemed honest, if not especially repentant. Her stomach clenched. She couldn't let herself hope too much too soon. Admitting he was wrong and agreeing to change were two different things, and he hadn't exactly said he wanted them to have any kind of future—

"So, if you understand a little better now how it feels to have someone else run your life, where do we go from here?" she asked, almost afraid to hear the answer.

He threw his hands up in surrender. "Oh, no, darlin', I ain't steppin' into that trap."

"What trap?" Her pulse ran wild in her temples.

"The trap where you ask me what I want to do next and I answer what I really want and then you light into me like a bear tearing into a beehive for not letting you have an equal say in things."

"Gee." She pushed her windswept hair out of her eyes. "I guess you did get my point."

"Like an arrow between the eyes," he muttered.

"But I don't see how we can hope to work anything out businesswise—" She dipped her gaze to the tumbling yellow weeds whipping around their ankles. "Or otherwise—if we can't talk about what we both want and expect."

"Makes sense." He coughed into his fisted hand. "You go first, though. Maybe you should start with telling me how deep I am into this rodeo school and why you even picked it to begin with."

"Actually, you're not in it at all. It's just an idea I had. This land next to Price's spread was for sale. I knew it would be a good investment for you and help his business as well."

"Yeah, but why a bull-riding school?"

"What else would you teach, Cub, doily making?"

He chuckled.

She stuffed her hands in her jacket pockets. The tall weeds whisked at her pant legs as she moved a few steps closer to Cub and the weathered barn. "Besides, you know the old saying about a rodeo cowboy and ranching…"

He cocked an eyebrow at her. "What old saying? Never ask a cowboy the size of his spread?"

If he intended to appear menacing, the effect went awry.

He seemed the picture of charm and amusement to Alyssa, which only unsettled her a little as she pressed on. "The saying 'Ask ten cowboys what they want to do when they stop rodeoing and you get the same ten answers—'"

"Open a bull-riding school?" he asked before she could finish.

"Ranch."

"This doesn't look like a ranch to me, Alyssa." He moved to her side. He took one moment to squint at the banner again, then fixed a hot, teasing gaze on her and whispered, "Unless, of course, you plan on breeding bull-riding cowboys."

Mentally, she stepped back, but physically, she could not move. She knew she must use her wits to push him away before he saw the hunger his suggestive tone and words provoked in her. She lowered her lashes and worked her voice into the best sneer she could imagine under the circumstances. "And I suppose, *you're* volunteering to stand at stud, cowboy?"

"Well, it *is* my name on the banner, there, darlin'." He grinned.

"And I also imagine you've already got a whole stable of females just waiting to…accommodate you." The sneer sounded real now, and tinged with pain.

He shifted his hips. His jeans, fitting like a second skin, rustled against his boot leather in the quiet. "If that's your way of asking me if I've slept my way through the rodeo circuit these last three years, then the answer is no."

"I wasn't—" Then again, she thought, maybe she was. If she was totally honest with herself, she had to admit it had crossed her mind time and again, the idea that Cub had been with other women, many other women. "It's none of my business what you did while we were apart, Cub. After all, you thought our marriage had been annulled and you had every right—"

"But I didn't," he said with quiet conviction as he inched close to her.

"Of course not." She put her back to him, still unable to get her feet to pad out a retreat. "You were injured, after all."

"Injured? Hell!" He huffed through his nostrils. "I got a hip out of whack, gal, not the whole damned lower region. *That* still works just fine."

His boots shuffled closer. She felt the roughness of denim against the soft fabric of her pants.

He fit himself closer still. "Thought you might have noticed one of those times you helped me with my physical therapy."

She had noticed. Just as she noticed now.

"It wasn't my...injuries...that kept me from any midnight rodeos with buckle-chasing cowgirls." He put his hand on her shoulder and dipped his head to whisper in her ear. "It was you."

"I'm sure I don't know what you mean." Her upper arm tensed under the warmth of his grip.

"I'm sure you do."

She twisted her head and narrowed her eyes at him. "So, you're saying these last three years, you've lived like a monk?"

"I'm saying I got up out of bed one morning nearly three years ago and kissed my wife goodbye. I had no thought or desire of making love with any woman until I was lying in her arms again."

Their gazes met. Their shoulders touched. She felt his heart thudding against the taut muscles of her back. His hips crushed into the rounded flesh of her bottom.

"Nothing ever changed that, Alyssa. You asked me what it was I wanted to do next, and if I answered honestly I'd say, I want to crawl into bed and lose myself inside you until we've loved away all the years of hurt between us."

"Cub," she murmured. "We can't just fall into bed and hope that solves all our differences."

"I know that, Alyssa." He rubbed a strand of her hair

between his thumb and forefinger. "I also know that I'm never going to stop trying to prove to you that you can count on me, that I'm a worthy man to share your bed—and your life."

"Oh, Cub."

The softness in her eyes made Cub's throat tighten. Slowly, so slowly the process left an ache though his body and heart, she was coming around. Maybe, he thought as he slid her shining hair off her shoulder, his hope for them wasn't misplaced.

"You don't have to prove anything to me. I know you're—"

"Mama, the baby gots a pony!"

They both jerked their heads up to see Jaycie astride a gentle old nag coming through the nearby pasture with Price leading the animal by the bridle.

"Hi, Mama!" Jaycie gave a floppy wave as Price pointed the horse to them. "Baby good pony rider. Pony mine."

Alyssa snatched at her jacket collar and turned on Cub. "I know you're a dirty, rotten sneak! Cub Goodacre, how could you?"

"How could I what?"

"Get your friend to let Jaycie think she can have that pony." She flung one arm out to point to the toddler jouncing atop the sway-backed mare. "You set me up for this!"

"I did not."

"Don't." She shut her eyes and shook her head. "Don't even bother trying to deny it now. The whole time I was here trying to—"

"Go ahead, say it, trying to set *me* up, that's what this bull-riding school baloney was all about, wasn't it?" The sting of being falsely accused dampened his libido in a flash and hardened his rasping voice. It was one thing to take his licks when he was truly at fault, but to know she couldn't even give him the benefit of the doubt? That was something he had to rail against. "You brought me here to set *me* up. To give me a visual aid as to how bad a husband I've been. So you have no call to go blaming me, Alyssa, especially since I didn't do a darned thing."

"Didn't do a—? Are you denying you arranged for Price to take Jaycie out so she'd think she was getting a pony?"

"Hey, you're the one who keeps telling me that Jaycie makes up her own mind, and I haven't seen any evidence to the contrary, darlin'." He gripped his hands on his hips. "You knew as well as I did that Price was taking her horseback riding. You should have seen this coming."

"Oh, so now it's my fault?"

"Whoa." Price brought the horse to a stop, careful to place a hand on Jaycie to keep her from toppling off. "Sounds like we came at a bad time, li'l stuff. Maybe we should take another lap around the pasture."

"No," Cub and Alyssa chimed in unison.

At least they agreed on something, Cub decided as he waved away the discord with a flick of his wrist. "It's not a bad time, Price. We appreciate your taking her out so Alyssa could show me my...surprise."

Price chuckled and handed the reins over to his friend. "So, what did you think about it? You gonna hang up your chaps and let us start callin' you Professor Goodacre?"

Cub laughed but kept his opinions about that to himself. "Like I said, thank you, Price. Now, Jaycie, time to get down and go home."

He reached up to put both hands around his daughter's middle.

"No. No go." She wriggled in his grasp. "My pony."

"Here, let me." Alyssa shouldered him out of the way, her hands raised to the child.

"I can take care of this, Alyssa." He kept his fingers curved around the toddler's back and stomach. "In fact, I think the time long past due for me to step in and help handle things with the baby."

"But—" Alyssa dropped her hand to the back of the saddle.

"No." Jaycie clutched at the saddle horn. "Want stay on the horsie. My pony. Mine."

"It is not your pony, little lady. It never was and it never will be." Cub used an even tone, much like talking to a high-strung horse. "And I'll tell you why it won't be."

Whether she understood his words or his tone simply soothed her, Jaycie quieted enough for him to get a good grip on her. Just in case he'd managed to reach through the thirty pounds of self-involved terrible two-year-old, he went on with his explanation.

"First, your mama doesn't want you to have the pony."

"Oh, great, make me the bad guy," Alyssa muttered.

"And second, *I* don't want you to have the pony."

"You don't?" Alyssa tilted her head to one side.

"Not anymore."

As if trying to reason with him, or perhaps just using some technique learned in the womb for wrapping a daddy around her finger, Jaycie pushed out her lower lip and said, "Me want pony for mine, pwease."

Cub fought against his raging guilt and the unfiltered cuteness of his own little girl. "With your grandparents always indulging you and your mama wanting to fuel your independent streak, you're running every risk of becoming a grade-A brat, Miss Jayne Cartwright Goodacre.''

At the mention of her name the child blinked at him, her huge eyes looking straight through him.

He half expected some kind of denial or at least a well-aimed piece of sarcasm from Alyssa. When none came, he went on. "I wouldn't be much of a daddy if I let that happen and I wouldn't be much of a daddy if I didn't let you learn that we don't always get the things we want most in life.''

Alyssa's fingertips went white against the saddle.

He wanted to look at her, to try to convey all his pain and longing in that look, but didn't dare. It wrenched his gut to disappoint them both like this. He knew how much Jacyie wanted a pony and he knew that by being the one to tell her no, by jumping in and taking charge, he was blowing it big-time with Alyssa. Still, it had to be done.

"Your mama and I don't agree on the reasons, darlin', but both of us agree on this, no pony.''

He pulled her off her mount, her legs kicking.

"No. My pony.'' Fat, angry tears welled up in her eyes; her entire face went red.

When he pulled her small body to his chest, she scowled at him between sobs and jabbed an accusing finger at his nose. "Him's not funny.''

"No, I reckon I'm not one bit funny to you right now, baby girl.'' He held her firmly but gently, his hand cupping the back of her head. "But that's fine with me. I don't give a hoot if you think I'm funny or not. I'm your daddy and it's high time all of us started acting like it.''

# Chapter Ten

Jaycie's anger had lasted about as long as the car ride back to the ranch. Alyssa's was another story.

Cub paused to listen for her footsteps in the hallway. She had kept a rigorous schedule these past three weeks for his daily physical therapy. Today, however, she was half an hour late and he'd begun to wonder if she would come at all.

"I overstepped my bounds, kiddo," he told his daughter, who was toddling around him like a drunken imp as he knelt on the den floor. He flattened his palms to the thick braided rug beneath them. "No doubt about it, I'm in the doghouse."

"Yours no doggie." Jaycie patted him on the forehead.

"Thanks, sweetie."

"You pony!"

Cub chuckled. "That's right, baby, I'm your very own private pack pony. Unfortunately, where your mama is concerned seems I'm just another cowboy-hat-wearin' jackass.''

The instant the term left his lips, Cub wished he could take it back.

"Please,'' he whispered between his teeth, his gaze following the redheaded child as she pretended to comb her "pony's'' mane. "Please don't pick up the one and only thing I've said today that would get me in more hot water with your mama.''

Jaycie patted his arm as if to console him. Moving in front of his head, she squatted down, her tiny jeans bunching as she looked directly up at him. Her chubby cheeks rounded up in a delighted grin. She raised her tiny finger in the air.

Under his breath, Cub said, "Call me funny, call me princess, call me anything but—''

"Jackass.''

He shut his eyes. "*That* you can say perfectly.''

"You jackass.''

He sat back on the heels of his boots, poked two fingers into his breastbone and said, "Daddy.''

"Jackass.''

"No.'' He wagged his finger at her. "I'm Daddy.''

"You jack—''

"No!''

The sharp command startled her. She peered up at him, wide-eyed, as if trying to decide what to do next.

"Please, Jaycie, darlin', why can't you just call me Daddy?'' He ran one hand back through his hair, which had gotten shaggy over the last few weeks, then urged again, "Try. Just try to call me Daddy.''

She opened her mouth. She closed her mouth. She puckered her lips, scrunched up her nose and stared at him.

"Daddy?" he coaxed.

She stood and charged up to him, tugging on his arm and insisting. "Pony."

"Fine." He got back on all fours. "Call me pony. At least it's an improvement over—"

"Well, it looks like you two sure made up real fast." Alyssa leaned against the door frame and smiled down on father and daughter. "Guess Jaycie just can't stay mad at you."

"Like mother, like daughter?" he asked, knowing that in this case they did not share the trait but thinking it might lighten the mood.

Before Alyssa could answer, Jaycie slapped both her hands on Cub's ribs and proclaimed, "My pony!"

He bent one arm to help the tot onto his back, grinning as he said, "Guess it's kind of hard to stay mad at your own personal live-in pony."

Jaycie nabbed Cub's shirt collar, kicked her bare heels against his sides and let out an earsplitting, "Hee-haw!"

Cub hobbled around on his knees a few steps, gritting his teeth to combat the discomfort of his every move. When he couldn't take another step, he pretended to rear up, his hand holding the child protectively in place.

Alyssa started to laugh at his antics but she must have seen his fleeting wince and she stopped.

"Cub! No!" Alyssa rushed forward and in one swift movement had caught up Jaycie and pulled her from Cub's back, telling him, "That can't be good for your hip."

Both father and daughter began to protest but she cut them off with a slash of her hand through the air. "I don't want to hear it. It's time for Jaycie's nap and your therapy, anyway."

Cub got to his feet, disguising his usual groans of effort with amicable laughter. "Yes, ma'am."

"Tell Daddy you'll see him after your nap, Jaycie." Alyssa moved the toddler on her hip so that the child could easily see Cub.

Jaycie pouted.

"C'mon, darlin'," Cub pleaded, his face level with the child's. "Say it for me. Say see you later, Daddy. See you later Daa-deeee."

"See you yater—" She lifted her hand in a wave, then a devilish grin broke over her face and she concluded, "jackass."

Alyssa shut her eyes.

Cub braced himself to bear the brunt of another tongue-lashing, to be reminded once again that he messed up even the simplest things.

A long sigh eased though Alyssa's lips.

Cub tensed.

She turned her head and pinched the baby's chin. "Looks like I'm going to have another long talk with your grandpa about cussing in front of you."

"Actually, Alyssa, I—"

"She picked that word up from Daddy five or six weeks ago and every now and then it just sort of pops out."

"You mean, it's not my fault?"

"Not unless you told her to call you that."

He looked at Jaycie, pretended to wipe sweat from his brow and winked. Of course, the baby had no idea what he meant but she giggled anyway, extending her hand to him.

Cub kissed the small, wriggling fingers. "See you when you wake up, baby."

Alyssa moved through the doorway, then turned to

look at him with a stern expression he didn't for one moment buy. "And I'll see you in ten minutes in your room for your therapy session."

"Looks like you've already started your warm-up stretches." Alyssa swaggered into Cub's bedroom with all the bravado of a lady warden. She didn't smile. She didn't joke. She wore an oversize black sweatsuit and pulled her hair back in a frazzled ponytail to accentuate the severity of the situation.

She'd adopted a no-nonsense attitude to remind them both that all the necessary touching and physical contact required of Cub's therapy was part of the job of getting him better, nothing more. If only she could convince her own body of that.

She watched Cub, seated shirtless on the floor. He bent his head and rubbed one hand over his shoulder and neck.

Despite all they had suffered, seeing him—his rippled muscles, the dark hair accenting but not obscuring his chest and abdomen, his hard, life-worn body—made Alyssa shudder. He affected her more each day she came here to help him, because each day she felt her defenses weakening. Each day she spent with him, she realized that if he was not yet fully changed in his attitude toward her, he had begun that process.

Today, his reaction at the phony bull-riding school, his admitting that he'd been wrong and his standing up with her as a parent to say Jaycie could not have a pony had only heightened her response to him. She'd delayed starting his therapy as long as she could, hoping to clear her head, to steel her resolve, but now, looking at him like this, she realized it hadn't worked.

Cub extended his arms in a long stretch, then stole a

quick glance up at her. "We're late getting started today. You still want to go through the whole session?"

She crossed her arms. "Well, if you don't think you're up to a whole session..."

The thin scar on his jaw lengthened as his lips curved into a sly smile. "I'll give you a whole session and then some, darlin'."

A tiny quiver, starting in the pit of her stomach, radiated through Alyssa's body at the potential of that promise. She really had no business being here today—not unless she intended to go through with the next step in rebuilding their relationship. She laced her arms beneath her aching breasts and leaned back against the door, ready to dart away.

"I've been working some on my own," Cub said, getting into position on the rug for his first series of warm-ups. "Watch this."

Cub's legs, in dark green sweatpants that bagged low on his hips, stretched open before him as he strained to reach further and further forward. When his fingertips touched the carpet just past his open knees, he looked up at her.

"Not too shabby, huh?"

"Your hip flexor flexibility has certainly improved." She hoped that sounded clinical enough.

She retreated to the doorway, her gaze skimming every nuance of Cub's exposed body. She flipped her ponytail to create a cool breeze on the back of her damp neck.

He straightened, bracing himself with his hands behind him, and grinned at her. "Some improvement, huh? I think I'm going to come out of this in better shape than I've been in years."

*No argument here.* She blinked. Had she said that

aloud? Cub's unchanged expression gave her hope she had not. She shut her eyes. She had to get out of here before temptation finally overcame her. She'd been too long without this man and too long in trying to reconnect with him to risk it all on quick—but sweet—sexual gratification.

"Um, I just remembered something I need to do." More like something she needed to *not* do, she told herself. She needed to not let herself get into vulnerable situations with this man until their future was settled, one way or another. She held her hand out as she stepped backward. "Keep exercising, Cub."

He said something back but she didn't hear; her heart hammered too hard in her ears. She spun on her heel and took one stride away when a sharp cry from Cub made her freeze.

He cursed.

She rushed to the doorway. "Are you okay?"

"Go on, I'm fine. It's just a cramp in my thigh—I overextended without warming up. Don't worry about it."

Alyssa held her breath and for a split second watched Cub grabbing at his thigh, grimacing. If she crossed that threshold now, given her weakened defenses, her heightened desire for this man, she knew she would commit herself to more than helping him with a short-lived spasm.

He raised his face and scowled at her. "Go on, gal. The last thing this cowboy needs or wants is your pity for his battered old body."

"And that," she said, raising her chin and stepping across the threshold, "is the last thing you're going to get."

This was his own little piece of cowboy hell. Cub

leaned back and closed his eyes. His teeth clenched until his jaw throbbed as Alyssa dug her fingers into the cramping muscle in his thigh. For most men, being alone in a bedroom with a beautiful woman kneading their thigh with supple fingers would be paradise. Not for Cub.

Too busted up to ride, living under the same roof with his wife and daughter but denied being a husband or daddy. Now given a massage by the woman who had filled his sexual fantasies for three years only to realize it was strictly therapeutic.

Top that off with the realization that to show her he'd really changed, to prove himself worthy to her, he had to show her that he could postpone his own wants, that he could put her needs before his. That only equaled pure hell in his mind.

"Cub?"

"Hmm?" He didn't dare look at her.

"I'm not being too rough, am I?"

The sultry breathiness of her question made him wish he had on tight jeans instead of the flimsy sweatpants draped over his hips and legs. He raised his other leg, hoping to create a baggy camouflage for the evidence of his response to Alyssa's touch.

"No." His whisper cracked mid-croak. He cleared his throat. "You're not too rough. Not rough at all."

"Good." She worked up his leg, following into the hollow along his tensed backside. "Feels like you're all knotted up."

"You have no idea," he muttered, knowing she meant his muscles, not his libido.

"Maybe we should skip the exercise therapy today then." The bed dipped as she climbed fully onto the mattress next to him. On her knees, she bowed her head.

A strand of strawberry-blond hair slid forward, dangling over her nose and mouth and touching her chin, practically begging him to sweep it away.

Her teeth scraped across her lower lip and she said, "Maybe what you need is a good, thorough rubdown."

Her fingertips scored from his outer thigh inward.

He shot his hand out to grab her by the wrist. "Actually, I think that's enough massaging, darlin', I'm a lot better."

"But you still seem…tense." She gazed at him in a full, sexual pout that had him far beyond tense.

"Alyssa, I don't know what you're trying to do, but it isn't relaxing me." He scooted back against the headboard as much for support as to ease away from her tempting caresses.

She placed one hand on his thigh and leaned over him, bracing her upper body over his with her other hand on the headboard. "Cub Goodacre, just how stupid do you think I am?"

"Is this a trick question?" He cocked his head, dragging in a deep breath rich with their mingled scents. "Because, darlin', you know I do not think you are stupid. But my guess is, you're trying to make an entirely different point."

"Entirely different." She swung one leg over both of his to straddle his lower body. "Did you think I didn't know what I was doing when I offered you a massage? I'm not some innocent young girl, waiting for a man to show me what to do anymore, Cub, in business…or in bed."

"That so?" A pang of jealousy ripped though his chest. It had never occurred to him that someone else might have contributed to her "physical education" in his absence, but now he wondered.

"That's so." She flattened her palm to his naked chest.

"And how—" He had to ask, even as his throat closed around the thorny question "How did you get so 'smart'?"

"I learned from the best." She placed one finger on his chin.

"Yeah?" He drove the straining lump in his chest down with a painful swallow.

"Yeah." She leaned in, her lips parted, her gaze always in his until she came so close her words tingled over his own mouth. "I learned everything I know from you."

Despite its gentleness, the kiss consumed him like a flash fire over parched ground. More than the sensation of the woman he loved kissing him, touching him, rocking her body against his, the pure emotion of the moment, of the very act, made him wild with desire. Alyssa wanted him. After all this time, after all the ways he'd failed her and come up lacking, she still wanted him.

She pulled away and gazed down at him, her moist lips red and full as she took a long, shuddering breath.

"Darlin', you say you know what you're doing, and damned if it doesn't feel like you do." He gripped her by the hips to still the mind-racking contact as she swirled her body in seductive slow motion against him. "But didn't you tell me earlier today that we couldn't just fall into bed and hope to work out our problems later?"

"If we wait until all our problems are worked out, Cub, we'll be ninety years old before we ever make love again." She smiled as if she'd just taken a straight shot of tequila. "Marriage is a work in progress, a partnership where both people help each other grow and learn in order to build a relationship and a future.''

"And?"

"And I've seen that willingness to work together in you, Cub. In the way you've been since you came to the ranch, in your reactions today, even in the fact that you would stop me from making crazy passionate love to you just to be sure it was the right thing for us."

He raised an eyebrow, wet his lips and dug his fingertips into the resilient flesh of her hips. "Did you say make crazy, passionate love?"

"Yes, but I wouldn't want to force you into something. If you're not ready..." She moved her leg to climb off of him.

"Oh, no, you don't." He held her in place. "I've been ready for this for a very long time."

She traced one finger along his jaw, down his neck and over his collarbone.

He sucked air through his teeth. His skin pebbled in a million tiny goose bumps.

"There's one thing I do want to know before we go any farther, Cub." She flicked the edge of her thumb over his dark, flat nipple.

He shut his eyes and groaned in pleasure. "What is it, darlin'?"

"If we do this, it's another step toward rebuilding our marriage, right? If it's not—"

He gripped her teasing fingers in his and lifted his head to bury his intent gaze in hers. "It is. I never wanted to stop being your husband, Alyssa. That was never what our differences were about. But I do want to deserve to be your husband."

"You do." She cupped his face in her hands. "You

did deserve it and much more than I gave you with my selfish behavior."

"Naw, I—"

"Cub, if you never did anything more than love me, trust me, be my friend and my lover, be a real father to our baby—or our babies—you'd deserve my love and devotion and so much more than I can even express."

He almost believed her. "It means a lot to hear you say that, darlin'. But you left out one important thing."

"What's that?"

"I've got to help you, not run things for you, but help you just like you help me. If I didn't do that I wouldn't deserve you, or the baby or your love or any of it."

"Oh, Cub." Her lips came down on his so softly he wondered how, with all the hunger and power of the moment surging in his body, he could maintain that kind of quiet intensity in their lovemaking.

It was wasted worry.

Sweatclothes, he realized as Alyssa began tugging away his pants and allowing him to pull off her shirt, might not be as a sexy as tight jeans, but they were a damned sight easier to be rid of in an emergency. That's what this felt like, a rush of urgency so strong it bordered on dangerous, which only added to its appeal.

Knowing Alyssa felt the same immediate needs only fueled his actions as he tossed his pants and her shirt from the bed. Even as his fingers flew to the cord holding her pants up, his wife peeled off her lacy bra to reveal the rounder, fuller breasts motherhood had bestowed on her.

The sight made Cub groan and work all the faster to release her from the constraints of her clothing so he could rediscover her curve by curve, inch by inch. The tie undone, he slid his hands inside both her pants and panties to cup the bouncy fullness of her behind.

She moved to allow him to push them down. She whisked them from her sexy, tanned legs then paused, kneeling over him, both of them naked and ready. "Is this the best way for you, for your hip, or should we—"

He clasped her waist in his hands and brought her down until her damp warmth met his steely hardness. "This is good."

She smiled and leaned forward, her hair falling to tickle his cheek, his nose. Her full breasts bobbled against this hairy chest and he edged his hands upward to take them, to rub his thumbs over the rosy pink centers.

She mewed like a kitten, then gave him a look that was pure wildcat. "Guess it's time for me to cowboy up and see if you can hang on for more than eight seconds, partner."

If he'd ever been happier, he didn't know when. Odds were, he realized as she fit herself to him, shut her eyes and took him in one deep thrust, if he ever was any happier than at this moment, it would kill him.

He found her rhythm fast, then tried to slow her, to make their reuniting last, but she fought his attempts. To his delight, she took over completely, leaning down to bite at his neck while she bucked against him in unrestrained desire. Small sounds, half caught in the back of her throat, sent him higher and harder, his whole body shaking in need for release.

"Darlin', I can't hold back—"

She cried out his name again and again and he needed no further encouragement to join her in the explosion of ecstasy.

A long, lazy moan escaped her lips as she tumbled forward to lay her head on his chest. "That was..."

"I know." He tangled his fingers in her hair.

"I guess this means you'll be moving from the guest room to my room?"

"Yeah." He sputtered a mellow laugh. "Soon as I *can* move."

She tenderly kissed the scar on his jaw. "We're going to be a real family, aren't we?"

A family. The idea warmed him like some sappy Christmas song on a cold lonely night. "Yes, we'll be a family. You, me and the—wait a minute, darlin'."

"What?" She pushed her chest and shoulders up, bracing herself against him. "What is it?"

"Things got pretty involved pretty quick here and I'm afraid there's one thing we didn't think about."

"Only *one* thing we didn't think about?" Her cool fingertips brushed his temple. "And what was that?"

He smoothed his hand down her bare back. "Everything between us is still so new and—well, adding another baby to the mix right now..."

"Oh." She held her lips in a perfect circle which grew into a knowing smile. "Ever since I had Jaycie, I have learned a lot about my body and how it works and I can tell you, it's no guarantee, but I don't think I'm in my fertile period."

"That's good." He blew out a true sigh of relief. "Not that I wouldn't want us to have more children— when the time is right."

"I understand." She shut her eyes and nuzzled his neck again. "Still, maybe we should make a trip to the drugstore before next time."

"Gee, you think we have time?" The onslaught of

pleasure in her delicate nibbling stirred his blood all over again.

To prevent an instant replay—with emphasis on the "instant"—of their fevered lovemaking, he took her hands from him and guided her naked body off his. "Okay, let's make that trip, and then 'next time' we'll take it nice and slow and make it last a very long—"

The shrill ringing of the telephone cut him off.

"Let the answering machine get it," she whispered as she reached down to scoop up their clothes. "That way we won't waste any precious time."

It rang again.

"Woman, I like the way you think." He accepted his things from her, his eyes drinking in her inviting body. "I also like the way you—"

"If you're calling for Jacob Goodacre, you got the right number. Leave a message."

"Good thing I didn't expect you to open a *charm* school, cowboy." Alyssa laughed and shook her head at his greeting.

*Beep.*

"Hey, Cub? Gosh, I wish you were there." Shelby Crowder's voice felt intrusive and grating to Cub, especially under these circumstances.

He jerked his sweatpants on, determined to ignore it.

Alyssa's head popped through the neck of her sweatshirt. She blinked at Cub. "Why is Shelby calling you?"

"I did some checking like you asked."

"You asked him to do some checking? On what?" She stood, hitching up her pants as she did.

Her anxious stare only made Cub hurry all the more to pull on a shirt so they could get out of there.

"Man, I've made so many calls on your behalf I feel like the phone has grown to my ear."

Cub yanked his shirt over his shoulder, nabbed his boots in one hand and pushed open the bedroom door. "C'mon." He extended his free hand to her. "Let's get going. I can listen to this later."

She took one hesitant step toward him.

"You were right, the value of the ol' Cub Goodacre name has skyrocketed with just about everyone associated with bull riding." Crowder hooted a hard laugh. "And I was able to use that as leverage to get a huge bump from your sponsor for the last ride in New Mexico."

She froze.

"It's just like you said, pal, it's like winning the lottery, the lotter—"

Cub lunged for the phone. The minute the receiver lifted, the answering machine cut off.

"The lottery?" Alyssa folded her arms, tiny sparks of static electricity in her sweatshirt prickling as if to punctuate her hushed tone.

"I—" He put the phone to his ear.

"Cub, how could you?"

"Hang on, Crowder." He placed the receiver to his chest. "How could I what? Take charge of my own career?"

"*I* was supposed to be in charge." She stabbed one finger into her breastbone, her hurt-filled eyes awash with unshed tears. "I had everything under control. You haven't changed one bit."

He narrowed his eyes, his grip tightening on the phone. "You know better than that, Alyssa. You said yourself I'd proven to you how much I'd changed."

"If you really want to prove to me how much you've changed, Cub, hang up that phone." Her lower lip trembled but her tears did not fall, her voice did not waver.

"Walk away from bull riding before they have to wheel you away from it."

He blew a short blast of hot air through his nostrils. "I can't do that."

"Not for my sake? Not even for Jaycie's?"

"It's for you two I have to make that ride, Alyssa." He could see in her eyes that she did not understand and he felt helpless to make her do so. "And, I won't lie to you, for my sake as well. You said some pretty strong things about marriage being a partnership. Well, in my book that means both of us contribute. This ride and all the money associated with it is my contribution to our future, Alyssa."

"Don't pull the noble cowboy, doing-what-he-must routine on me, Goodacre. I had enough of that show three years ago." One tear slipped onto her cheek and rolled down. She left it. "If you insist on risking your health to make that ride, I don't see that you and I have a future."

"I'm sorry you feel that way." He turned his back and slowly raised the receiver to his ear. Above the sound of Alyssa rushing from the room and down the hall, he said, "You have my full attention, Crowder. Tell me what I have to do."

# Chapter Eleven

"**M**ine!"

Alyssa stared at the open door near the end of the hallway. Cub's room, where Jaycie had gone earlier to play with her daddy, not knowing she had also gone to say goodbye, beckoned to Alyssa.

For four days she and Cub had hardly spoken, hardly been able to make eye contact. Now he was preparing to leave, packing up to head out for a last round of medical tests and the promotional appearances that would culminate in his last ride.

The very term made her shudder. Last ride. Her eyes stung and her stomach churned. How could a man be so arrogant, so full of pride as to risk everything on eight seconds? Eight seconds that could leave him permanently disabled—wealthy but disabled, she corrected.

He said he was doing it for her. The savvy businesswoman in her understood and appreciated his point. To forfeit this ride would ruin his reputation, ruin any hope for the future earning power of his name. He'd become just another busted-up cowboy limping away from the rodeo circuit. That could ruin her own business as well, by dashing their hopes of big commissions and by associating the Crowder and Cartwright Management Company with the collapse of a short but brilliant career.

He said he was doing it for Jaycie. As a mother, she appreciated his need to provide a good role model, to follow through on his commitments, to do his best and give his all. But, her heart argued savagely, if Cub gave his all to the rodeo, what would be left for her and their child?

Anger welled again in her chest. She shut her eyes and wound her fingers into the weave of her shapeless brown sweater. Suddenly, she wished he'd never come back to Summit City, never sought her out again, never seen that picture of Jaycie in his darned old cowboy boots.

"No, bad, bad. Mine. Mine!" Jaycie's frustrated cries brought Alyssa back to the moment, to the reality of Cub's leaving. She used her revived anger to push her forward, storming to the bedroom door.

"Oh, for goodness' sakes, Jaycie. Let him keep his darned old cowboy boot—"

It wasn't the pair of battered boots that had the tiny redhead in distress, Alyssa realized the moment she stepped into the room. She blinked to clear her vision as she watched the child struggle to push away the very suitcase Cub was attempting to pack.

"No, no," the toddler said, shaking her head in desperate fury. "Bad."

Cub sank to the bed beside the open case and distraught child. "Honey, I told you, Daddy will be gone only a little while. Then I'll come back and I'll bring you a present."

"No present." Jaycie broke into a plaintive wail, throwing herself into her father's arms and sobbing, "Mine! Mine!"

Cub buried his face in the child's hair and Alyssa thought she heard him sniffle as Jaycie croaked out, "Baby wants him to stay. Him's mine."

"Looks like this is one of those times you talked about," Alyssa said, moving over to stroke the wispy baby curls on her daughter's head. "One of those times when she has to learn she can't have everything she wants."

Cub nodded without looking Alyssa in the eye, then lifted the baby into her waiting hands. "It's a lesson that will serve her well in life."

Alyssa pulled Jaycie close and the child whimpered.

Cub rose as slowly as he had when his hip had been at its worst, turned and fastened the suitcase latches with a final snap. "I guess I've got enough packed for the trip. If you don't mind, I'll be leaving some things here."

"Sure." She glanced at the plain western shirts in his closet, knowing he would have taken only the showiest ones for his exhibition. Below them, the old boots that had brought them together lay on their sides, probably just as Jaycie had left them when she last played with them.

She noticed that the framed photos she'd given him of the baby no longer sat on the dresser. He'd want to take those, of course, though he had left the yellow flyer, still folded just as she'd seen it in his hotel, along with some loose change in an unused ashtray. His cane remained, propped up in the corner of the room.

"Guess it's goodbye, then," he said, his gaze on the baby, not Alyssa. "I'll be back, darlin'. Bye-bye."

"Say bye-bye to Daddy, sweetie." It amazed Alyssa that she had the breath to get the sentence out, much less sound calm and upbeat.

Jaycie raised her hand.

Cub touched his fingertips to her plump tummy.

"Bad." The child slapped his knuckles with a quick crack. "Him's very bad."

"He's not bad, honey, he's your daddy," Alyssa whispered through her growing pain. She wished the whole scene would end so she could get back to her life without Cub. With that in mind, she cleared her throat and urged, "Please, just tell him bye-bye."

"Bye." Jaycie raised her hand. "Bye-bye—"

"Daddy," Cub supplied for her in a strained murmur.

"Jackass." The child tipped her chin up.

"Jaycie, no, that's not nice." Alyssa saw the hurt in Cub's eyes for only a second before it went cold and he reached for his hat.

"Don't bother correcting her on that, Alyssa. I know it's a sentiment you probably share." He pushed down the smoky brown hat with the cattleman's crown and Aussie brim until it covered his eyes from her view. His cheek went taut, his voice raw, "Like mother, like daughter, right?"

He grabbed the suitcase, then pushed past her and out the door.

"If you're calling for Jacob Goodacre, you got the right number. Leave a message."

Alyssa took her finger from the playback button on Cub's answering machine and the tape whirred to rewind itself. The message light showed no calls had come in during the two weeks he'd been gone. She'd come here for that reason, she told herself, to check his messages—as a favor to him.

Why then, she wondered, had she lingered in the dimly lit room, savoring the scent of the man, which grew fainter every day? Why had she shut the door to give herself privacy to replay his recorded voice again and again? Why, then, did she wish she could throw herself down on the bed, the place they'd made love in what seemed a joyous reconciliation, wrap herself in the sheets that last touched his skin and cry herself into a merciful dreamless sleep?

She could not—or would not—answer herself. Neither would she look herself in the eye in the big mirror in front of her. She sighed and let her gaze tumble from the answering machine to the toppled pair of boots in the closet. Even Jaycie had lost all interest in playing with those boots since her daddy left them behind. Alyssa wondered if it was possible that the once loved boots could have become a symbol to the child of Cub's abandonment—just as they had once been for her.

Well, she'd gotten over that, just as Jaycie would. In fact, not so long ago the trauma of Cub's leaving had been so far removed from Alyssa's heart that she had used those boots to launch her very own bid for independence.

Angling her chin up, Alyssa reached for the flyer, folded in quarters, lying in the pristine ashtray. The single page crackled as she unfolded it, her eyes fixed on the adorable picture of Jaycie in cowboy gear and Cub's boots. She smiled, then glanced over the rest of the copy.

"Not bad for a first try at PR," she told her image in the mirror, trying to bolster her own spirits. "Even if I do say so my—"

She blinked at the reflection of herself and the backside of the flyer. Writing, not just any writing but a letter in familiar script, shone back at her.

Her heart stopped.

"My letter," she murmured, trying to figure out why and how it had come to be in Cub's possession. She lowered it with trembling hands, trying to make herself recall if he had said or done anything that might indicate he'd read her message cast into the wind.

"He couldn't have," she quickly concluded. If he had the letter and wanted to keep it a secret, he would not have left it behind. If he hadn't wanted it kept a secret, then she'd have known about it, no doubt about that.

Suddenly, she remembered the day he'd found the flyer on her porch, folded it and tucked it in his pocket. That was the day he learned about Jaycie. So much had happened, in fact, since that day, she doubted he'd given the wayward flyer a second thought.

"Too bad," she whispered, turning it over to read the first words of her own heartfelt plea.

Dear Cub
Come home.

A sharp gasp of air cut through her aching chest as she skimmed along the words hastily scrawled on the paper.

Though I realize I will always love you in that wild, intense way that suits a reckless cowboy like you, I have to let go of the dream that we could ever become equal partners in a relationship.

"Liar." She arched one eyebrow at herself in the mirror. "You never let go of that dream. You still haven't or you wouldn't be in here, looking for some clue, some reason to believe..."

She sighed and scanned further along in her letter. Past the story of trying to find Cub and the effect of the birth of their daughter, she read on, her pulse quickening as she compared her thoughts then to her heartache now.

What will I tell our daughter when she is old enough to ask about her father?

She read near the close of her letter.

...that her father was a good man with a great capacity to love but a very narrow definition of what that meant.

How wrong she'd been to think that. If she ever doubted how immense Cub's definition of love had become, she need only think of his treatment of Jaycie, his drive to do what was best for the child he hardly knew, but loved without reservation. She shook her head. If she ever doubted Cub's love at all, she need only think of his determination to make this damned last ride to keep her business solvent.

Why did he have to be so stubborn? Why couldn't he have just let her handle things? The small endorsements she'd arranged wouldn't stave off the problems her company might face if Cub broke his contract to ride Diablo's Heartbreak, but he'd be safe. Why couldn't he just accept her judgment and be safe?

She swallowed hard, glancing back at the letter through a blur of tears.

*He thought he could save me from my own mistakes—and that was the biggest mistake of all.*

Her own words, her own scathing assessment of Cub mocked her from the yellow page.

"That's it, isn't it?" she asked her bleary-eyed image. "I wanted—no, I demanded—a chance to make my own mistakes, then denied him the same consideration."

She folded the paper back into neat quarters, as what felt like the weight of the world settled on her shoulders. "Who has the 'very narrow definition of love' now?"

What the hell was he doing in New Mexico? Cub rubbed his callused hands over his face, trying to force himself to concentrate. In twenty-two minutes he would make the ride that would leave him a hero or a goat in the eyes of his fans, sponsors and the record books.

And all he could think about was what he'd left in South Dakota. He lifted his eyes to scan the crowd, hoping against impossible odds to see Alyssa's face. He listened with a desperate intensity to hear Jaycie's excited "hee-haw" among the constant drone of voices.

Who was he kidding? He lifted his hat from his head, smoothed his hand through his hair, then resettled the Cub Goodacre trademark down low.

"Everything in order, Cub?" A tall redhead with a "Rodeo Hospitality Volunteer" badge pinned precariously on her chest smiled at him.

"You mean, do I have my last will and testament dictated and signed?" He exhaled through his nose.

"Oh, c'mon, now, the outcome isn't that bleak," she teased.

"Tell that to my—" *Wife.* He'd almost said it, but at the last moment he caught himself. "Manager. There's a lot riding on this little eight-second bone-rattler."

"You're up to it. If any cowboy can best that bull,

it's you," she assured him, her gaze as adoring as her words.

"You think so?" His mouth quirked up on one side. With his eyes in shadow and that implied amusement, he felt sure she had no idea of his truly lukewarm response to her sexually charged enthusiasm, or the searing pain that lay beneath it. He sighed but it did not ease the weight of his weariness. "I wish everyone shared your confidence in me, darlin'."

"Just be sure, I'm rooting for you, Cub." She pressed her glossy lips together.

Cub braced himself for what he knew would follow. How many ways, he wondered, had he learned in the last three years to turn down a voracious buckle bunny? He'd used every excuse known to chump and champion alike, except the one he felt he'd never had a right to.

She swished back her almost monumental mane of hair and smiled at him like a cat toying with its prey.

"I was thinking," she said, "that maybe after your ride we could—"

"I'm sorry, darlin', I'm not interested. You see, I'm a married man."

She blinked and he didn't know whether she was shocked by his status or surprised he'd consider it a hindrance to their getting together. "You? You're married?"

"Yes, as a matter of fact he is."

*Alyssa.*

"To me."

Cub turned on his heel slowly, almost afraid he'd imagined the welcome voice from behind him.

"It's really you." He didn't give a damn how strained with emotion that hoarse whisper sounded; he felt every razor-sharp edge of it and then some.

"I'll be going now," the redhead said, every inch the gracious loser. "You need to be in the chute in fifteen minutes, Cub. You're going to do great."

He nodded a thank-you to the parting volunteer, his gaze never leaving Alyssa, who stood, feet planted firmly, head cocked, just a few feet away.

"Hello, Cub," Alyssa said, his name soft as a prayer on her lips.

He blinked in the shade of his hat brim, his eyes damp and warm. "You're here."

She crossed her arms over her black-and-red western shirt. "Where else would I be on the night of your big ride?"

"You mean because you're my manager and so much is at stake tonight?"

"I mean—" Her arms dropped to her side. Her cocky attitude dropped as well. She took two steps to bring herself close enough to touch and spoke in a choked murmur, "I mean because I'm your wife."

"Alyssa." He put his hand on her cheek, moved past his own agony by her simple profession.

She turned her face and pressed a gentle kiss into his palm. Then she reached to wad his shirtfront in her fist, pulling him closer still. "I was wrong, Cub, I was so wrong."

"No, it was me." He tipped his hat to the back of his head. "I really let you d—"

"Don't." She pressed her fingertips to his lips. "You've done anything *but* let me down, Cub. You couldn't have, because since you came back, you've done the one thing for me that I wanted all my life."

"Made you a mother?" He stroked his thumb over her cheek.

"No."

"Helped you start your dream business?"

She shook her head.

He cradled her face in his hands. "What, then? What did I do for you, darlin'?"

"You loved me."

"There's no denying that."

"And you loved me without trying to force me to be something or someone I couldn't be. You loved me without trying to impose your judgment on me, without criticizing me for not sharing your dreams, your goals for me." Her eyes shimmered with tears, her lower lip quivered as she took a shuddering breath and finished, "And I never even told you how much that meant to me."

He leaned in, just about to kiss her when she shut her eyes, slipped his hat from his head and whispered, "I love you, Cub Goodacre. I always have and I always will."

He filled his kiss with his response. Forceful yet tender, he took her mouth, folding her into his arms and pulling her to him so hard he feared he'd bruise her ribs. But she showed no signs of physical pain, instead digging her fingers into his arms as she opened her lips in an unreserved invitation.

She loved him. She'd come all this way to tell him—to *show* him—that. And he didn't deserve it, he never would. That was the crazy thing about love, he finally understood as he deepened the kiss and shared himself body and soul with his wife. Love wasn't earned, it just *was.*

"Oh, Cub," Alyssa whispered as they drew apart.

He put his forehead to hers. "If you ask me to, darlin', I'll forfeit the ride right now."

"I won't ask to do that, Cub." She moved her hand,

clutching his hat to put the smoky brown crown sideways between them. "But I will ask you this."

"Anything, Alyssa."

Her eyes lifted to search his. "When you ride tonight, don't do it for your mama, or me or Jaycie or any woman you think you ever let down in your life. You're a good man, Cub, and no matter what the outcome, you always tried your hardest and gave your best and that's all anyone can expect."

"I think I'm beginning to understand that, darlin'."

"Good." She smiled, lifted his hat and fit it down on his head. "Then go out there and ride for you. Make it a fitting tribute to the kind of cowboy you are, the kind of man you are."

"You mean a last hurrah?"

She bit her lip, hesitated, then asked softly, "Will it be your last?"

"Has to be."

"Is that what the sports-medicine specialists say?"

"No, it's what I say." He held her by the shoulders. "I've got too many dreams and responsibilities to stay out on the rodeo circuit any longer, darlin'. Not to mention a beautiful wife and a baby daughter who, for some reason, seem kinda fond of seeing this beat-up old face around the place."

"We sure do. Jaycie is at home with my folks counting the hours till you come back to her, I'm sure."

"She can count *and* tell time?" he teased.

"What can I say, our baby is a genius." She put her hand to his shirt. "She misses you, Cub. I did, too. There's just one thing I want to know."

"What?"

Her boots shuffled in the dust. She glanced away and

then back at him again. "Did you read the letter I wrote?"

"What letter?" He cocked his head and rubbed the fine stubble on his chin. "Did you write me a letter?"

"No." A slow smile worked across her sweet, beautiful face. "I think maybe I wrote it to myself."

"I don't understand."

"You don't have to. Just tell me this, after this ride, will you come home and make a new life with me and the baby?"

"I'd like to meet the man or bull who could keep me from it." He stroked her hair.

"But if you give up the rodeo, what will you do?"

"Well, there is that bull-riding school idea. Or I may take a notion to just make promotional appearances and endorsements and spend the rest of the time as a stay-at-home daddy. You're my manager—you tell me what I should do."

She grinned. "Start by showing old Heartbreak out there that he can't throw you ever again."

"I'll do that." He kissed her temple, then stepped back. "You going to watch this time?"

"Like this," she promised, lifting her hands to cover her face, then parting her fingers to peer through.

He laughed. "And when it's over, we'll celebrate."

She gave him a look that could melt his spurs. "Well, you know what the rodeo cowboys say, one good ride deserves another."

"And another." He grabbed her by the waist and stole a quick but fiery kiss before turning to head to the chute and his final farewell to Heartbreak.

# Chapter Twelve

"Coming up next it's the grudge match you've all been waiting to see, Cub Goodacre against Diablo's Heartbreak."

"That feller announcing a bull ride or a wrasslin' match?" Yip grumbled.

"Shh, Daddy. Do you want to watch the video of Cub's ride or not?"

"Just press the mute button, sweetie," Dolly suggested with a melodic wave of her hand.

Alyssa smiled at her parents nestled in the leather sofa of the family room of their ranch. "You mean Daddy has a mute button?"

Her mother tipped her head back and rolled her eyes, "Oh, don't I wish he did."

"Oh, hush, the two of you, and give me that remote control, it's almost time for the man's ride." Yip snatched the remote from Alyssa, perched on the arm of the sofa.

With the push of one big thumb, he cut off the announcer's voice and they were left to watch the taped version of Cub's now-famous ride. This time, however, Alyssa did not watch the heart-stopping eight seconds feeling on the verge of a panic attack. This time, for the first time ever, probably, she could see the grace and power and poetry of the sport and fully appreciate Cub's talent and grit in mastering it.

She watched as the camera came in tight to show Cub preparing for the ride, then giving the nod to say he was ready. The chute sprang open and Heartbreak blew out like a cannonball, his head low. Alyssa leaned forward, caught up in the moment as the crowd held a collective breath waiting to see if the bull would spin left or right or simply throw Cub like a rag doll into the air.

Heartbreak went left but Cub anticipated it, hanging on with one hand high over his head. The leather tie of his hatband whipped up and down as if goading the rider on to do better, to demand more of himself and the beast. In every other ride, Cub lacked the luxury of showmanship—it had been enough just to hang on. But this time it was different. He gave the crowd everything they could wish for from a champion, and then some.

"Six Mississippi, seven Mississippi," Alyssa counted under her breath just as she had that night a full week ago. "Eight—"

The buzzer went off. Cub had done it. The crowd paid him with an exuberance more precious than the oversize bank draft his sponsors had handed him at the conclusion of it all.

"What a ride." Yip slapped the sofa with an open-handed smack. "It's a damned shame you've got that boy retiring now just when—"

"Alyssa doesn't 'have me retiring,'" Cub stepped

through the doorway, his denim jacket collar turned up and Jaycie in his arms.

"Ah, now, I didn't mean she had you on a leash, son." Yip chuckled as if they were trail partners exchanging common knowledge. "Just that I can see my daughter's hand in this. You know that despite her best intentions she doesn't always make the right choices."

"She does fine." Cub handed the child to Alyssa, then placed his arm around her shoulder showing a united front.

"Let me handle this," she whispered to her husband, proud of his willingness to defend her independence but wishing to exercise that independence herself. "Daddy, Cub makes his own decisions and so do I. Whether you agree with them or not, or whether we agree with each other for that matter, doesn't make those decisions any less valid."

Yip pushed up from the couch to loom over them, not in an angry way but in that great, big daddy's-in-charge-here way he had about him. "What in land's sake are you talking about, missy?"

"I'm talking about running our own lives, the way we see fit. It's time I stood up to you, Daddy, and let you know, you did a fine job raising me, but now it's over. I can take care of myself."

Yip's face went red. He blustered something that wasn't quite a cough or a cussword.

"Sounds an awful lot like a speech you gave your own daddy not long after we were married, Clarence." Dolly rose. With a delicate jingle, she patted her husband's arm.

Cub ducked his head to hide a grin.

Alyssa bit the inside of her cheek to keep from breaking out in a triumphant smile herself.

"Guess this means you won't be buying the baby a pony for sure now," Yip grumbled.

"Pony!" Jaycie clapped her hands in glee.

"Well, actually—"

"Well, sir—" Cub and Alyssa spoke at once. He tipped his head to encourage her. "You tell him."

Alyssa set the baby on the ground. The little one squealed and ran from the room headed, no doubt, for some familiar part of the house to find a plaything.

"You see, Daddy, Cub would like to try his hand at ranching," she began tentatively.

"He would?" Yip scowled.

"Nothing big, just a few head, maybe run a bull-riding camp on the side," Cub explained.

"That can be an expensive proposition to get going…"

Before her father could make the offer to help financially, Alyssa spoke up. "Cub can afford it, the setup and the upkeep until it turns a profit, don't you worry about that, Daddy."

"Besides, you know what they say—'Behind every successful rancher is a wife with a steady job.'" Cub winked at Alyssa.

The sight and the vote of confidence made her spirits soar. She snuggled against Cub's side and sighed. "The upshot of all this, Daddy—and Mama—is that we've bought a piece of land bordering Price Wellman's place. We're going to build a house there."

"And stables," Cub added.

"And we'll have some cattle and, of course, horses."

He placed one finger under her chin. "And a whole bunch of kids."

She could only smile back at him like the crazy-in-love woman she was. "And we're going to let all those kids decide for themselves what they want to become, not try to shape them into images of who we think they should be."

"Whether they want to be cowpokes or accountants." Cub gave her a squeeze.

"Sounds perfectly lovely," Dolly said. She dabbed at her eyes with the lacy sleeve of her blouse.

"And how does all this highfalutin talk fit in with my granddaughter getting herself a pony?" Yip crossed his arms.

"Oh, Daddy." Alyssa laughed and rolled her eyes. "Jaycie will have her pony—when she's old enough to help take care of it. I mean, I could try to keep her from being a rowdy cowgirl but that would work about as well as trying to—"

"Turn her mama into a sequin-wearing, jumping-through-a-flaming-hoop, trick-pony-riding rodeo queen. Right, Alyssa?" He looked down at her, his own eyebrow cocked.

She laughed again. "That's right, Cub. I'm afraid our baby was born to the breed, just like her grandpa and her daddy."

And if she needed any further proof of that, in came Jaycie herself, galloping full force on a stick pony. Cub's old boots scuffed and clomped as the baby wearing them ran a circle around her parents.

She pulled back on the reins of her imaginary pony, stopped and bellowed out an earsplitting, "Hee-haw!"

"That's my girl!" Yip beamed at the child.

"No." Cub stepped forward and scooped up the girl, holding her high between her mother and himself. "That's *my* girl."

"Me my girl." She stabbed one finger into her chest.

"You tell him, Jaycie." Alyssa patted her child's back.

"Me, mine. Mama, mine." She stuck one booted foot out. "Boots, mine."

For a moment, Alyssa saw the longing in Cub's eyes, the unspoken hope that he, too, would be claimed by his child.

"Grandpa, Gandma, mine."

That put a sparkle in Yip and Dolly's eyes to rival anything in their wardrobes.

Then Jaycie turned. Every eye focused on her, all waiting to see if she would at last acknowledge Cub.

He drew in a deep breath.

Alyssa struggled not to whisper the right words, to coax them from her child's lips.

"Him…" Jaycie poked one finger at Cub.

*Mine.* The desire of everyone in the room to hear her say it made the word seem almost audible.

"Him…" she said again, a grin breaking slowly over her entire face. "Him, Daddy."

Jaycie threw her arms around Cub's neck and Alyssa followed, Cub closing his girls in a tight embrace.

"That's right, sweetie," he said in that broken, sexy, beautiful voice of his. "I'm your daddy. And I love you more than my next breath and I love your mama all that much and more."

Alyssa's eye met his above the crop of red curls. "I love you, Cub Goodacre. I always will."

\* \* \* \* \*

# Take 4 bestselling love stories FREE

## a FREE surprise gift!

## Special Limited-time Offer

**Mail to Silhouette Reader Service™**

3010 Walden Avenue
P.O. Box 1867
Buffalo, N.Y. 14240-1867

**YES!** Please send me 4 free Silhouette Romance™ novels and my free surprise gift. Then send me 6 brand-new novels every month, which I will receive months before they appear in bookstores. Bill me at the low price of $2.90 each plus 25¢ delivery and applicable sales tax, if any.* That's the complete price and a savings of over 10% off the cover prices—quite a bargain! I understand that accepting the books and gift places me under no obligation ever to buy any books. I can always return a shipment and cancel at any time. Even if I never buy another book from Silhouette, the 4 free books and the surprise gift are mine to keep forever.

215 SEN CF2P

| Name | (PLEASE PRINT) | |
|------|------|------|
| Address | Apt. No. | |
| City | State | Zip |

This offer is limited to one order per household and not valid to present Silhouette Romance™ subscribers. *Terms and prices are subject to change without notice. Sales tax applicable in N.Y.

# BEVERLY BARTON

### Continues the twelve-book series— 36 Hours—in April 1998 with Book Ten

# NINE MONTHS

Paige Summers couldn't have been more shocked when she learned that the man with whom she had spent one passionate, stormy night was none other than her arrogant new boss! And just because he was the father of her unborn baby didn't give him the right to claim her as his wife. Especially when he wasn't offering the one thing she wanted: his heart.

For Jared and Paige and *all* the residents of Grand Springs, Colorado, the storm-induced blackout was just the beginning of 36 Hours that changed *everything!* You won't want to miss a single book.

### Available at your favorite retail outlet.

# MEN at WORK

*All work and no play? Not these men!*

## April 1998

### *KNIGHT SPARKS* by Mary Lynn Baxter

Sexy lawman Rance Knight made a career of arresting the bad guys. Somehow, though, he thought policewoman Carly Mitchum was framed. Once they'd uncovered the truth, could Rance let Carly go...or would he make a citizen's arrest?

## May 1998

### *HOODWINKED* by Diana Palmer

CEO Jake Edwards donned coveralls and went undercover as a mechanic to find the saboteur in his company. Nothing—or no one—would distract him, not even beautiful secretary Maureen Harris. Jake had to catch the thief—*and* the woman who'd stolen his heart!

## June 1998

### *DEFYING GRAVITY* by Rachel Lee

Tim O'Shaughnessy and his business partner, Liz Pennington, had always been close—but never *this* close. As the danger of their assignment escalated, so did their passion. When the job was over, could they ever go back to business as usual?

## MEN AT WORK™

Available at your favorite retail outlet!

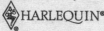 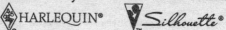

# This April
# DEBBIE MACOMBER

## takes readers to the Big Sky and beyond...

# MONTANA

At her grandfather's request, Molly packs up her kids and returns to his ranch in Sweetgrass, Montana.

But when she arrives, she finds a stranger, Sam Dakota, working there. Molly has questions: What exactly is he doing there? Why doesn't the sheriff trust him? Just *who* is Sam Dakota? These questions become all the more critical when her grandfather tries to push them into marriage....

Moving to the state of Montana is one thing; entering the state of matrimony is quite another!

Available in April 1998 wherever books are sold.

MIRA

MDM434

# SOMETIMES BIG SURPRISES COME IN SMALL PACKAGES!

**Celebrate the happiness that only a baby can bring in Bundles of Joy by Silhouette Romance!**

## February 1998
### On Baby Patrol by Sharon De Vita (SR#1276)
Bachelor cop Michael Sullivan pledged to protect his best friend's pregnant widow, Joanna Grace. Would his secret promise spark a vow to love, honor and cherish? Don't miss this exciting launch of Sharon's *Lullabies and Love* miniseries!

## April 1998
### Boot Scootin' Secret Baby by Natalie Patrick (SR#1289)
Cowboy Jacob Goodacre discovered his estranged wife, Alyssa, had secretly given birth to his daughter. Could a toddler with a fondness for her daddy's cowboy boots keep her parents' hearts roped together?

## June 1998
### Man, Wife and Little Wonder by Robin Nicholas (SR#1301)
Reformed bad boy Johnny Tremont would keep his orphaned niece at any price. But could a marriage in name only to pretty Grace Marie Green lead to the love of a lifetime?

**And be sure to look for additional BUNDLES OF JOY titles in the months to come.**

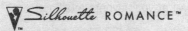

**Silhouette ROMANCE™**

Find us at your favorite retail outlet.

Look us up on-line at: http://www.romance.net

SRBOJF-J

# DIANA PALMER
# ANN MAJOR
# SUSAN MALLERY

## RETURN TO WHITEHORN

In **April 1998** get ready to catch the bouquet. Join in the excitement as these bestselling authors lead us down the aisle with three heartwarming tales of love and matrimony in Big Sky country.

A very engaged lady is having second thoughts about her intended; a pregnant librarian is wooed by the town bad boy; a cowgirl meets up with her first love. Which Maverick will be the next one to get hitched?

### Available in **April 1998**.

Silhouette's beloved **MONTANA MAVERICKS** returns in Special Edition and Harlequin Historicals starting in February 1998, with brand-new stories from your favorite authors.

Round up these great new stories at your favorite retail outlet.

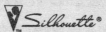

Look us up on-line at: http://www.romance.net

PSMMWEDS